ONLY HER CHRISTMAS MIRACLE

Mystical Lake Resort Romance #9

CAMI CHECKETTS

Birch River
PUBLISHING

COPYRIGHT

Only Her Christmas Miracle: Mystical Lake Resort Romance #9

Copyright © 2020 by Cami Checketts

Edited by Daniel Coleman and Ceara Nobles

DEDICATION

To my parents who always made Christmas a special miracle.

FREE BOOK

Receive a free copy of *Seeking Mr. Debonair: The Jane Austen Pact* by clicking here and signing up for Cami's newsletter.

PROLOGUE

Ashley Casey shifted uncomfortably on the tissue-covered fake leather bed in the dermatologist's office. An ugly rash marred her torso, arms, and legs. She not only itched like a dog with fleas, but she looked awful too. She was coordinating a wedding tomorrow night. A wedding she'd been working on for six months. She couldn't go to the elite event covered with hives —or whatever these nasty bumps were.

She pulled the flimsy robe tighter around her legs, tucking it under her thighs to try to minimize the exposure of her backside. The nurse had allowed her to keep her bra and underwear on, but that was it, so the doctor could see how severe the rash was. She'd been to this dermatologist before and the doctor was a classy, fifty-something lady who exuded kindness and knowledge. At least it wasn't some hot young doctor coming in to examine Ashley in her underwear. How awkward would that be?

There was a rap at the door, and she called, "Come in."

The door swung wide and her heart faltered. A dark-haired

man in a white medical coat holding a laptop paused in the door-way. His blue eyes swept over her, coming to rest on her face, and the most incredible smile split his too-handsome face. A well-trimmed beard highlighted lips that were full and ultra-appealing.

"Dr. Hamilton?" a female voice questioned behind him.

"Oh, excuse me, Mary." He strode confidently into the room with a nurse, apparently Mary, following. Extending a hand to Ashley, he said, "Dr. Chase Hamilton. Pleasure to meet you, Miss Casey."

Ashley registered the pressure of his warm, firm, manly hand surrounding hers, but she couldn't register that *this* was Dr. Hamilton. He released her, still giving her that incredible smile as he waited for her to respond.

"Uh ... wait ... who are you?" she stuttered in disbelief.

"Dr. Hamilton." His smile didn't falter, but his gaze went to her neck and then her arms. "Hmm. That is a nasty rash. And it's all over your body?" He stepped in closer as if he'd take her robe off and check all her body parts covered in angry red bumps.

Ashley gasped, pushed her hands down on the robe barely covering the top of her thighs and said, "You're not *my* Dr. Hamilton."

He paused and met her gaze again. Dang, his eyes were a fabulous shade of true blue. Why couldn't she have met this guy at one of her events? She'd be all dolled up in a fancy dress and in her element. He'd be impressed and interested in her. They'd talk. They'd flirt. As the event ended, she'd walk out to her Atlas and he'd follow her.

No! She needed a mental face slap. No way could she fall for another man. Seven fiancés was plenty on her record.

"Oh." He chuckled and she loved the melodious sound. "You're one of my mom's patients."

"Yes, I am. I would like to see *my* Dr. Hamilton, please." She looked past his handsome face and—dang, he was tall and nicely-formed as well—to the nurse who was giving her a bored look. "Where is the female Dr. Hamilton?"

"Let me think," Dr. Hamilton, the wrong one, answered before the nurse could, setting the laptop on the counter. "I think Costa Rica at the moment. As soon as I finished my active-duty commitments with the Army in October and agreed to take over her practice, she got it in her head to travel the world. She left a couple weeks ago and I don't know when she's coming back." He winked at her.

Ashley recognized the wink was friendly, not flirtatious, but dang if it didn't give her heart palpitations. What kind of doctor looked like a movie star and casually winked at his patients? This man was comfortable in his own skin and off-the-charts appealing to her. It made her even more aware that, at the moment, she was in this thin hospital gown and her skin was a horrific mess.

"Now..." Dr. Hamilton gave her another heart-stopping smile and moved in again. She caught a whiff of a manly, musky cologne that messed with her brain waves. "Are you comfortable with me seeing your rash and recommending treatment?"

"No!" she said much too sharply.

"No?" He drew back. His smile disappeared and a furrow appeared between his brows. "I apologize, Miss Casey, but my mother is currently out of the country. The receptionist should have informed you of the switch."

"She didn't."

He nodded and rubbed at the back of his neck. "Again, I

apologize. But I can also assure you I am a competent dermatologist, graduated with my doctorate and specialty from Yale, have
worked as a dermatologist for the Army for four years, and am
more than qualified to diagnose your rash."

"I'm sure you're very competent." She couldn't resist looking
him over and thinking he indeed seemed more than competent.
"But you have to understand that I was expecting a kind, classy
lady doctor. Your mother, who I'm comfortable seeing me in my
tighty-whiteys and then you—" she gestured to him— "walk in
all handsome and smelling good and ..."

His brows arched up.

"I just made this awkward," she finished miserably.

"Not at all." He was obviously trying not to laugh. "I promise
to be professional about seeing you in your 'tighty-whiteys.'"

She pushed the robe down under her legs tighter. "Oh, no
you won't, because it is not happening."

His eyebrows lifted. "Are you refusing treatment because I'm
a ... man?"

She gave him an imperious glare. "Don't you dare try to make
me feel bad for the big, strong, handsome military doctor."

Dr. Hamilton stared at Ashley, pinning her in place. If there
was ever a look so beautiful and appealing that made her want to
fling herself into some handsome doctor's arms, this was it. Was
she in an exam room or a sauna? She was hot all over. She'd been
engaged seven times and couldn't recall feeling this level of
attraction. Dang, she was a hot mess.

"Are you refusing treatment?" he asked quietly.

She was thrust back to the reality of her situation. She was
sitting half-naked on an exam table, covered with a nasty rash.
Almost on cue, she felt a horrific itch start on her abdomen. She
fought to ignore the need to scratch. She needed help, and his

mom wasn't here. She'd have to give the good-looking doctor a chance to treat her.

"I'm not refusing treatment," she said just as quietly. "Can you please recommend something for my rash?"

"I can." His confidence radiated from his smooth skin. He stepped in close, his firm abdomen brushed the outside of her leg, and his palm touched her arm. The warmth of his fingers penetrated her skin and soothed her rash. She wanted to beg him to touch her again and again. His gaze darted to hers and she was lost in a sea of blue. His fingers gently explored the skin of her forearm. He looked down and seemed to be studying it as he continued to run his fingers over the skin.

His gaze met hers again as he lifted both hands to the back of her neck, and then he started to untie the strings holding her gown on.

"What are you doing?" she shrieked, batting his hands away and holding the gown together.

His eyes registered confusion. "You gave me permission to examine your rash. I've just looked at it on your forearm, but your chart says it covers your chest, abdomen, and back."

"You are *not* examining my chest." She could hardly catch a breath. She should get out of here and just down Benadryl until the rash hopefully went away.

"Miss Casey." He sounded exasperated and offended. "I've already told you I'm a professional. I'm not trying to ... undress you."

Her cheeks flushed. She felt awkward and stupid. The nurse kept her gaze on the computer as if she was as uncomfortable as Ashley. This man was a doctor, and she was acting like he was a hot man trying to undress her. Well, he *was* a hot man, but he had medical reasons for needing to see her rash. Still ... she couldn't handle it.

"You can look at my legs and my arms," she insisted. "And ... my back, I guess, but you are *not* checking out my chest and abdomen."

He held up his hands in surrender, looking amused and frustrated at the same time. "All right."

"All right." She gave him what she hoped was a challenging look. This situation was already embarrassing. This handsome, appealing man was going to look at the disgusting rash covering her body and she was making it worse. To add insult to injury, her back was now itching as badly as her stomach. She clenched her fists to keep from scratching.

Dr. Hamilton looked over her arms and her legs and then came around behind her and lifted the thin gown away so he could look over her back. She shivered from the cool breeze and the knowledge that he could see her bra strap and the top of her underwear. She was being silly. He was a professional, but with the quiet nurse basically ignoring them, it felt as if they were alone and it was far too intimate. She tried to imagine he was old and ugly, but as his warm palm pressed against her midback right where the itch was, she sighed with pleasure.

"You're scratching it a lot," he stated.

How embarrassing was that? She probably had red scratches to go with the ugly bumps. Here he was, ultra-attractive, and she was a bumpy mess. "Yes," she admitted.

"Have you tried any creams or oral Benadryl?"

"I've been taking Benadryl since yesterday morning when I woke up and looked awful."

"You couldn't look awful if you tried," he said softly.

She darted a glance over her shoulder at him. The look in

those blue eyes was incredible. Could she possibly be as appealing to him as he was to her?

He cleared his throat and asked, "And creams?"

"Oh ... creams." Her mind was far from the rash. She wrung her hands together. "I've tried all kinds of lotions and over-the-counter creams. I even smeared Aquaphor over my entire body."

His eyes lit with a soft smile. "That probably felt a little greasy."

"Ruined my favorite shirt," she admitted.

He chuckled. "I can imagine." He lifted his hand from her back and walked around in front of her again. "I'll have Mary call in prednisone that will be taken orally and a hydrocortisone cream and antibiotic cream that you can apply topically as needed. The rash should be gone in a few days."

"A few days?" Her voice pitched up anxiously. "No, no, no. The wedding's tomorrow night."

"Wedding?" His brow squiggled.

She gestured to her bumpy arms and then pulled down the flimsy gown enough for him to see down to her collarbone and her shoulder. "My dress is off the shoulder. I can't have this nasty rash everywhere."

"Wedding," he repeated, his gaze suddenly cool and appraising as he studied her.

"Don't you have anything that will work quicker?"

He shook his head. "A rash can take weeks to clear up."

"Weeks? I can't look like this for ... Please." She grasped his arm. His very firm, very nicely-muscled arm. And got completely distracted from the stress of her rash. Their gazes met and got tangled up. The moment stretched beautifully. He was the first one to look away and break the spell.

She released his arm. "Please, there must be something to take it away."

He shrugged and said, "Some old remedies like a baking soda bath or an oatmeal bath might help soothe it, but only time and the oral and topical medications will remove it completely. I'm sorry about your ... wedding."

Why did he say wedding as if it was a public execution? Did this handsome doctor not believe in weddings? That actually made sense. Otherwise how could such an appealing, educated man not be married and have a few beautiful children by now? She glanced at his left hand. No ring, but that meant nothing. He might be married. She had to focus. The rash. Her dress for tomorrow's event.

"That's all you've got for me?" she asked desperately.

He flashed her a smile, but it wasn't as warm as before. "Find a dress with a high neck and long sleeves."

Ashley gaped at him. He turned and gave some instructions to the nurse about the specific medications to call into the pharmacy.

Turning back to her, he nodded and said, "Nice to meet you, Miss Casey. Good luck with your ... wedding." Again, he spat out wedding as if it was a naughty word. He tilted his chin, gave her one last lingering look, then he strode through the door and was gone.

Ashely felt strangely deflated, as if she'd just let someone leave her life who should've been a key part of it. That was silly. She straightened her shoulders and looked to the nurse. She'd take those prescriptions, and conquer this rash by tomorrow night.

Find a dress with a high neck and long sleeves.

She harrumphed. Pompous doctor anyway. But she could still

hear his voice as he said, "You couldn't look awful if you tried." A warm tremor ran through her. She wished she'd met him in different circumstances, and that he wasn't a wedding hater.

Oh, well. The perfect man for her didn't exist. Seven attempts and seven times running away in a panic was enough evidence of that. Her primary focus now was bringing true joy for her brides on their special day. She'd never have that day herself. Especially not with the handsome likes of Dr. Chase Hamilton.

CHAPTER ONE

Ashley rushed around the gorgeous Mystical Lake Resort in the remote mountains of Montana. The opportunity to coordinate not just one but three weddings for well-known, accomplished couples—as well as the gathering party for the Chadwick family and guests, and the Christmas Eve celebration the day after the weddings—was thrilling. After ten years of hard work, starting in her parents' garage before she even graduated high school, she was now the premier wedding planner in middle Montana. It felt great.

The premier wedding planner who'd run the wrong way down the aisle seven times.

Well, that wasn't exactly true. Most of the times, she'd dumped the groom well before the big day. As it turned out, she had more fun planning her wedding than actually participating in it, especially because each of her fiancés had revealed themselves to be flirting cheats at one time or another. She sure knew how to pick them.

She didn't need a man, or a groom, or a guy anything. The only man who constantly invaded her thoughts was the handsome dermatologist who'd made her skin tingle. His treatments had cleared her skin up after a few days, but she'd had to wear a dress with long sleeves and a high neck to the event, as he'd suggested. Sadly, she hadn't seen him—besides in her mind—for four long weeks. It was just as well. He'd gotten really awkward when she'd said the word 'wedding.'

She hurried into the open main area of the resort, thinking about the hundred things she needed to do before the meet-and-greet party tonight. It was December twentieth, and the breathtaking main building of the resort was decorated with a dozen trees, greenery, and lights everywhere. But the natural decorations outside of snow, pine trees, mountains, and the frozen lake were prettier than anything manmade.

She hurried toward the front desk to see if the attendant knew where Catalina Chadwick Stillwater was. Cat's partner and cousin, Iris Chadwick, was one of the brides and the first wedding that would take place tomorrow evening. Ashley had tried to bug Cat on any last-minute details and problems so she wouldn't give the bride any extra stress. Rumors were flying about a huge snowstorm that might keep the out-of-town and even the valley wedding guests from making it to the resort tomorrow evening. It was enough to give Ashley stress for all of them.

A tall, well-built man with a trimmed beard and a confident set to his shoulders waited for the elevator. It dinged open and he walked inside. Turning, he pushed the button and then his gaze lit on Ashley. A gaze with bright blue eyes set in a handsome face that immediately had her heart racing. All wedding worries evaporated from her brain.

"Dr. Hamilton," she murmured.

"Miss Casey," he said as if she was the last person he expected to see standing there.

The door slid closed and he was gone. Ashley stood there in shock for half a second. She shouldn't chase after him, but ...

She forgot all about Cat and her questions as she ran for the stairs and then pounded up to the second story. Glancing out into the hallway, she saw no one. She ran back to the stairs and up to the third story. Another check. Nothing.

There were only two more stories, but the good doctor may have already gotten to either floor four or five and disappeared around a corner or into his suite. She sprinted up to flight four, panting for air, her legs burning. The beautiful, tall, manly man walked down the hall and turned the corner, disappearing from view.

She shouldn't have chased him. Obviously, he didn't care to push the button to stop the elevator, open the door, and talk to her again. Cursing herself for chasing a man who wasn't interested, she rushed down the hallway. She simply wanted to see where he was going. She also wouldn't mind talking to him when she wasn't his patient... or covered in a nasty rash.

Hurrying around the corner, she spotted him. She stopped and planted her back against the wall, leaning around to see him and hopefully not get caught.

The door swung open and a throaty female voice squealed, "There you are! Get your handsome body in here with me. I'm about to make all of your dreams come true."

Ashley's body deflated. Dr. Hamilton disappeared into the room. He was with someone. Dang and yikes, that woman had been ... forward. Maybe it was his wife and Ashley had no business eavesdropping. What did Ashley know?

She shook her head and trudged back to the stairs. She'd hit an all-time low. Chasing a man who was in a serious relationship, possibly married. This was why she'd vowed to stay away from men. She was only interested in flirtatious jerks. Dr. Hamilton was obviously in a relationship, and he'd been flirting with Ashley. Okay, maybe she'd only imagined he'd flirted with her. It was par for the course.

———

As the elevator doors closed on the main lobby and Chase could no longer see Miss Ashley Casey's lovely face, his shoulders rounded. He wanted to hit the button to stop the elevator and demand to know if she was married, if it had indeed been her wedding she'd been so worried about having a rash for. It had to be. Why would she have been so upset otherwise?

He forced away the memory of her smile, blue eyes, and beautiful face, as he had so often the past month. Otherwise he feared he'd find a way to track her down, maybe unethically look at medical records and find her address or phone number. He'd stayed strong, wishing she wasn't married and that he'd see her again without a nurse looking on and worrying whether he was crossing doctor-patient boundaries. It had been difficult to stay professional with how crazily interested he'd been in her.

Now he'd seen her again. She was staying in the very resort that he'd been lured to by "America's sweetheart" Kris Bellissima. He wasn't one to waste time on social media. If he wasn't at the office, he was snow-skiing in the winter and in the summer he was exploring trails on his bike or exploring caves, spelunking with some close friends from grade school on up, but he'd have to live under a rock to not know who Kris was.

When the infamous woman contacted him, asking him to meet her at Mystical Lake Resort during the Christmas holidays as she had news about his father's family that would "change his life," he'd been intrigued. His mom was still off in South America somewhere, enjoying semi-retirement with her close friend, Ned. Chase kept wondering when he'd hear they were engaged, or even better, married. He liked Ned. The man treated his mom great, and Chase wanted his mom to be happy. She'd never married, finishing medical school while expecting him and graduating two days before he was born. He'd never known a father, but his mom had always been there for him. They were as close as mother and son could be. He'd missed her the past six weeks, but he couldn't begrudge her finally taking some time for herself.

Most of his friends were off with family this Christmas and though several close friends and two army buddies had invited him to join them, Kris's offer had intrigued him. He'd Googled her. She was benevolent and well-loved by the media and the public. She'd been involved in a scandal last summer with the hockey player Quill Chadwick, but both had come off looking good. Another Colorado Avalanche player, Todd Plowman, had gone to prison for gambling and throwing a hockey game, and some entertainment writer named Pepper had taken the fall for printing lies about Quill.

Chase knew a little about the Chadwick family. They seemed like an impressive crew. He'd had a few people tell him he looked like the Chadwick brothers, and similar to the famous actor Bennett Pike, the man Cedar Chadwick was a stunt double for. He hadn't let his own speculation grow out of proportion as he'd given up on ever getting the truth about his father, but it was intriguing.

So here Chase was, at the famed Mystical Lake Resort, chasing information about his father's family. Kris hadn't said his father would be here, which honestly was a relief. From what Chase knew about him, the man was a scum who'd seduced his mom and left her high and dry when she turned up pregnant. Apparently, the guy had his own family somewhere else. So maybe Chase had a whole slew of step-people—or was it half-people?—connected to him. He'd almost called his mom to pry for details, but she hadn't given him any in the past thirty years. He doubted that would change now and he didn't want to upset her until he knew more about Kris's mysterious offer.

He'd wanted to spring back out of the elevator and talk to Ashley Casey, but he was already late for his meeting with Kris. He'd get it over with, see what information she had or if it was just another person who wanted to speculate that he looked similar to the Chadwicks. Maybe after, he'd go find Ashley. It couldn't hurt to talk to the beautiful woman, simply ask if she was married. If she wasn't ... he'd be here until the day after Christmas. If she was staying here, there might be some possibilities.

He rapped on the door to Kris's suite. She swung it wide and grinned at him even wider. She was a model-gorgeous woman, there was no denying that, but there was a predatory gleam in her dark eyes that made him wary. He liked the innocent light he'd seen in Ashley's blue eyes, but right now he needed to focus. Get the information, get out. Just like a military op.

"There you are!" Kris squealed. "Get your handsome body in here with me. I'm about to make all of your dreams come true."

Chase's eyebrows rose. He wanted to spring the other direction, but foolishly he let her lead him into the suite. Hopefully she thought his "dreams coming true" meant finding his father's family. When he was a small boy, he couldn't imagine anything better than having a dad. Well, a couple tough older brothers and a little sister were high on his list also, but he'd shut those dreams down when he realized how much they hurt his mom.

As the door swung shut behind him, louder than a coffin lid closing, he wondered if he should've insisted on meeting in a public place. Kris was wearing a silky red robe that clung to her shapely body. She tried to drag him to the couch. He stopped near the door and folded his arms across his chest.

"I appreciate you asking me here to give me information about my family." He got straight to the point, not wanting to give her any indication that he was interested in anything besides information.

Her plump lips turned down in a pout. "I was hoping we could get to know each other better before I told you *all* my secrets." She winked and gave him a sultry look, loosening the tie on her robe and giving him a glimpse of cleavage spilling out of a lacy black bra.

Chase's eyes widened and he backed toward the door. "Maybe it's smarter if we meet in a public place. I'll plan on the steakhouse for lunch at one."

He spun and grabbed the door handle, yanking the door open.

"I thought you'd be interested in more than just my information," she flung at his back. "Your brother certainly was."

"My ... brother?" He whirled to face her but stayed in the open doorway.

She walked slowly toward him, letting her robe fall off one shoulder. Chase backed into the hallway. If she took that robe off, he was running. He didn't believe in shallow hookups and this woman was giving him all the wrong vibes.

"Quill Chadwick." She leaned against the doorframe, tossing her hair so it spilled over her chest. She slowly undid the tie on her robe.

Nope. Chase was done with this interaction. He whirled and ran for the elevator. Her throaty laughter followed him. "You'll be running back this direction soon," she taunted.

Chase darted past the elevator and to the stairs, sprinting up one floor to his suite on the fifth floor. He shut himself in and deadbolted the door. He wanted to laugh at himself, the tough army doctor running from a small woman. But that woman was terrifying. What was she about? Had she only claimed to have information so she could seduce him? Why? She was a famous woman. He was good-looking and a lot of women liked the thought of dating a doctor, but there was no gain for someone like Kris Bellissima to undress for him. She was a renowned influencer who surely had a lot of men pursuing her. Was it some weird play to get back with Quill?

His mind focused on the information she'd tried to give him. Quill Chadwick was his brother? He paced the large suite, looking out the windows at the beautiful view. The mountains, snow, and trees did nothing to calm him. He couldn't believe anything that woman told him, but he wanted to pound on her door again, tell her to put some clothes on, then demand to hear her information.

Over the years, people had claimed he looked like Cedar Chadwick, the stunt double for the famed actor Bennett Pike, or Quill Chadwick who played for the Colorado Avalanche. He had several times wondered if that could be his father's family, but his mom had always redirected when he asked about his dad. If he persisted, she clammed up or even a few times locked herself in her bedroom. Out of respect for her, he had stopped asking.

Could it be possible? Why had Kris only mentioned Quill? What about his dad and his other siblings?

Chase was here now. Maybe over the next five days, he could get to know some of the Chadwicks. But even if he did, what was he supposed to say?

Hey, I think I'm your illegitimate brother and son and I've always wanted a brother and a father. You probably don't want me around, but can we hang out?

He should call his mom. He'd always assumed his dad was a junkie or a loser, but if he was the father of the impressive Chadwick family, he must be pretty amazing. The thought gave Chase a weird clutch of hope in his chest. He'd never seen anything about the Chadwick parents when he'd seen any of the brothers in the media.

He pulled out his laptop and went to trusty Google. There were quite a few pictures and even articles of Cedar Chadwick, the stuntman for Bennett Pike; Quill, of course, as the superstar of the Colorado Avalanche and when he was on the arm of Kris Bellissima last year; and their cousin Cruz Chadwick who had some incredible videos on snow skis and doing all manner of tricks on different boards behind a boat. There wasn't much about Aster besides that he owned a large construction company in Jackson Hole, and Ren, the youngest, was a smokejumper firefighter in California. There was one small article about Iris and Catalina Chadwick taking over the Mystical Lake Resort. He studied the picture of Iris for a long time. She was a beauty with long, blonde hair and blue eyes. Could he possibly have a little sister? The idea made his insides feel warm.

He scoured the internet, but he couldn't find anything about their dad. In one of the pictures of Quill after a hockey game, there was an older lady who must be his grandmother. She had a welcoming smile and a mischievous twinkle in her blue eyes. He liked her on sight. He thought he might've finally found a picture of the man who might be his father, but the tall, angular man with the distinctive blue eyes was Quill's uncle, Jay Chadwick. Catalina and Cruz's dad.

He did find an obituary for Lucy Chadwick, his maybe-siblings' mother. The obituary was glowing about her angelic status as a mother, wife, aunt, friend, and sister. It said she was survived by husband, Peter Chadwick, but that was it. He felt bad the Chadwick family had lost their mother. Where was their dad? Maybe Chase would find him this Christmas. But there was no guarantee this was even his family and not just some weird ploy by Kris Bellissima to seduce him.

He shook his head, walked into the bedroom of his suite, and changed into warm workout clothes. He wasn't going to sit in his suite and stew about it. He'd go on a hike and work some of this junk in his head out. He wished he could simply think about the beautiful Ashley Casey, but he was afraid she might be married, so that wasn't a great path either.

He wished his mom was home. This Christmas was looking to be a lonely flop.

CHAPTER TWO

Ashley woke early and went straight to the window. It was still dark outside. Too dark, even though it was five a.m. Snowflakes slammed against the glass.

Please don't let it be too bad for the wedding guests to get here.

She had a patio on her suite, so she shoved the door open— or tried to. The wind howled and she was immediately plastered by wet, heavy, cold snow. The storm had started last night as the welcome party was winding down and the Chadwicks were heading to their homes. They'd all hoped it would blow itself out. Apparently it hadn't.

Yanking the door shut again, she closed her eyes and prayed. It wasn't just for her and all the work she'd put into these perfect weddings. It was for Iris, Meredith, and Hope. Each bride was unique, beautiful, and sweet, and she loved them like the sisters she'd always wanted. She had two older brothers and they were great, but they weren't girls.

It was too early to start making phone calls and too early to start stressing, at least that's what she told herself. Pushing the stress away was tough. She put on a t-shirt and workout shorts and shoes and hurried out of her suite and down the stairs. The resort was filled to capacity, but it was spacious and beautiful and at five a.m., she'd bet she had the gym to herself.

Luckily, she was right. She spent some time on the rowing and elliptical machines and then did a circuit workout with hand weights, the cable machine, and even forced herself to do a set of burpees with each round.

By the time she finished, she was hot, sweaty, and tired, but she did feel more relaxed. Even if the snow messed up the plan, she would make it work. These brides were all great. They weren't going to flip out like some Bridezilla and blame Ashley. The welcome party last night had gone amazing and all she'd heard from the Chadwick family and in-laws or future in-laws was praise and gratitude. She had to believe it would all work out just fine.

She walked from the gym, past the spa, and spied one of the indoor pools. She used her key and went inside, disappointed to find the lap pool wasn't empty. She would've been tempted to strip her shirt and shoes off and swim in her sports bra and shorts. Turning, she would've left, but something about the man slicing through the water seemed familiar.

She crept closer. The man's build was incredible. His muscular shoulders and back were on fine display as his strong arms cut through the water. He had a trimmed beard, which she glimpsed when he turned for a breath. He was in a good rhythm and didn't seem to notice her. She crept closer still, hoping, praying it might be Chase Hamilton. He hadn't chased after her yesterday and after that woman pulled him into her room, she shouldn't be hoping to see him now.

She was at the edge of the pool when he did a kick turn and surfaced. He stood—the lap pool was only five feet deep—and tugged off his goggles. Those blue eyes and that handsome face. It was definitely Dr. Chase Hamilton. His scrubs and doctor jacket had covered his broad shoulders the first time she'd met him. Nothing covered them now. Wow. Swimming had done that body good.

"Ashley," he said with a smile. "What are you doing here?"

"What am I doing here?" What right did he have to act like she was the one out of place? She straightened and glared at him, folding her arms across her chest. "I'm the wedding coordinator for three brides this weekend. What are you doing here?"

"Wedding coordinator." His eyes grew thoughtful for a few seconds and then a huge smile spread across his face as if she'd just handed him the cure for skin cancer. "You're a wedding coordinator?"

She nodded, wondering why he was so happy about it.

"So when you came to my office, you weren't worried about your skin looking good for your own wedding but for somebody else's?"

"My own wedding?" She put a hand to her chest. She'd planned her perfect day and thought she was marrying the perfect man. Engaged by Christmas and a spring wedding. Seven years in a row. She was definitely a slow learner, but she wouldn't make the same mistake again. "I'm not married."

"That is fabulous news." He rubbed his wet hand across his bearded cheek. "Brilliant news."

"What does it matter to you?" she demanded. He had walked willingly into that room with that woman yesterday. The lady who was going to "make all his dreams come true." Ugh! Why was he acting so happy that Ashley wasn't married?

He shrugged and the impressive muscles in his shoulders flexed. "Are you going to swim?"

"I just might, Dr. Hamilton."

His eyebrows rose but he corrected softly, "It's Chase to you."

She swallowed. She wasn't about to be that familiar with him, especially with the recent memory of him being led into that suite with the woman who wanted his "handsome body" in the room with her. His body was plenty handsome, but Ashley did not need another fake-charming, handsome, flirtatious, cheating man on her hands. Seven of them had been quite enough, thank you very much.

She gestured with her hands. "Go back to swimming. I don't need you watching while I get in."

He smirked at her. "Call me Chase and I'll think about it."

Ooh, he was infuriating. "Go swim."

He arched an eyebrow and folded those beautiful arms of his across his chest.

She gritted her teeth to stop from drooling and then finally added, "Chase," just so he'd swim and let her get in without him watching.

He grinned. "Thank you."

Ashley ignored him, sitting on a chaise lounge by the pool and untying her shoelaces. She should go back up to her room and get her swimsuit on, but she would only get in for a few minutes to cool off and de-stress. Maybe float on her back and not worry about weddings and parties and Dr. Chase Hamilton. As she yanked off her shoes and socks, she glanced up. He hadn't gone back to swimming as she'd instructed. The handsome man was still studying her. Not thinking about Dr. Hamilton might be difficult indeed.

She stood, tilting her chin imperiously as if him watching didn't bother her in the least, and walked across the rough concrete and then down the pool steps. The lukewarm water felt great. She was overheated from her workout, the stress of the storm coming to mess up her weddings, and the perfect-looking doctor staring at her.

"You're going to swim in a t-shirt and shorts?" he asked.

"What's it to you?" she countered, plunging under the water, t-shirt and all. It kissed her cheeks and cooled her heated forehead and neck.

She rose back up. The five-foot deep lap pool covered her up to her neck and her black fitted t-shirt revealed nothing, thank heavens. She'd shown Dr. Hamilton plenty in that flimsy gown when she had a thick rash covering her entire body.

He chuckled as she emerged. "If you want to take your t-shirt off, I won't look."

"No, thank you, Dr. Hamilton," she said primly.

He swam quickly up to her. She didn't move, but her heart rate ramped up. Stopping right in front of her again, he stood. He was tall. At least half a foot taller than her five-six. The last time they'd been this close, she'd been sitting on a doctor's table.

His gaze traveled over her. "I see a lot of skin in my profession. I'm not going to gape at you if you take your shirt off and swim in your sports bra."

She leaned back to gaze deeper into his blue eyes. "Well, you might see a lot of skin, but you're not going to see my skin."

He smiled and then laughed. "I promise I'm not trying to undress you."

"Just like you weren't trying to undress me in your office last month?"

"Exactly." He raised his eyebrows, all imperious and doctor-like.

In a flash of embarrassment, she realized what was going on here. She was insanely attracted to this man and he obviously didn't reciprocate the feeling. Of course it wouldn't bother him to see her skin; she was simply another patient.

"Did your rash clear up okay?"

"Yes." Exactly. All he cared about was a follow-up on her skin care.

"In time for the wedding?" He tilted his head; his blue eyes studied her intently.

"No."

"What did you do?"

She glared at him again. Why were they having this conversation? Where was the woman who had pulled him into her room yesterday? She admitted, "I took your advice and wore a dress with long sleeves and a high neck."

He chuckled. "Smart girl."

"For taking your advice?"

"Yes." His gaze swept over her. "And covering up that beautiful neck and those smooth arms."

Heat flushed her neck. Maybe he did find her attractive. It was a moot point. She had promised herself she would never be with a flirtatious cheater again, and she'd watched him walk into that room with that woman only hours ago.

"A professional opinion, Dr. Hamilton?" she asked.

"It's Chase," he said softly, taking a step closer. He was close enough that she could've brushed the smooth muscles of his chest with her arm if she chose to.

She needed to get away now or she'd forget he was here with another woman. What a jerk to be flirting with her when he was with someone else. Maybe he wasn't even flirting with her, just like in his office that day. She was making something out of nothing simply because of the attraction she had for him.

Turning, she ducked under the water and swam away freestyle. An arm wrapped around her waist and she was hauled back against the beautiful chest of Dr. Chase Hamilton.

"What are you doing?" she sputtered, turning in his arms.

"Forgive me, Miss Casey, but I'd really like you to call me Chase."

She planted her hands on his chest to push him away, temporarily distracted by how perfect the smooth muscle felt under her fingertips.

His heart thudded quickly under her palms. He glanced down at her hands and then up at her. "Forgive me," he murmured again. "Can you call me Chase ... please?"

Her heart was racing so fast that she couldn't catch a breath. She forgot every worry as his large palms covered her lower back and pulled her in tight. Her hands moved as if they had a mind of their own, sliding across his chest muscles and then up to his broad shoulders. "Chase," she whispered.

"Thank you." He smiled, and then he bent his head and kissed her.

Joy and light exploded in her too-sensitive lips and traveled throughout her body. She lost herself, cuddling in tight against his firm chest and savoring each moment of his very beautiful, very thorough kiss.

When he pulled back, he smiled gently down at her. "Ashley," he murmured. His eyes filled with awe and his hands rubbed up and down her back.

"What are you doing?" she managed, confused and all stirred up by him.

"I have no idea." His smile grew. "I thought I'd be alone, but now I've found you."

He dipped his head to kiss her again, but it hit her like a sledgehammer. He wasn't alone. He was with some other woman. She ducked her head and his lips brushed her forehead.

"Ashley?"

"Let me go," she demanded.

He immediately released her. His gaze changed from wonder and tenderness to confusion.

"You have no right ..." she sputtered. She'd kissed him as surely as he'd kissed her. She hadn't kissed anyone since Brandon, her latest fiancé who she'd ditched at the altar last April, almost eight months ago. That had to be why this kiss had felt so incredible. It wasn't that she and Chase—rather, Dr. Hamilton—had some incredible connection that she'd never experienced in her short lifetime.

Shame rushed through her. Within hours of leaving Brandon at the altar, numerous people had texted and sent social media messages detailing all the different women he'd been cheating on her with. It should've made her relieved she hadn't married the scum, but it had only caused her more pain. Her previous fiancés had also been flirts and she was certain several of them had cheated on her. She must be attracted to that type of man like her mom had always feared. One thing she knew for sure: she would never be the "other" woman.

"Stay away from me," she warned, pushing through the water to the stairs.

"Ashley."

She ignored the pleading in his voice as she climbed out of the pool and grabbed a rolled towel on the stack nearby.

"Ashley." He climbed quickly from the pool and put a hand

on her arm. She looked up at him. His eyes were full of an apology, confirming exactly what she feared. He was with that lady. "I'm sorry."

"You should be," she hurled at him. At least he had the good sense to feel guilty.

He stepped away, his body going rigid.

Embarrassed at how strongly she was reacting and then angry that she was the one who was embarrassed, she wrapped the towel tight around her, swept her shoes and socks off the floor, and rushed from the pool. She glanced back through the glass door as she exited. Chase hadn't moved. He studied her with a furrowed brow, the muscles in his chest and arms tight. He looked amazing. He'd felt amazing. She was even more disgusted with herself. She wasn't into purely physical relationships and obviously he was. She felt pity for the woman who was probably up in his room waiting for him right now. What a jerk.

CHAPTER THREE

Chase alternated between angry and confused as he finished his swim, showered, and ate room service in his suite. How could Ashley have kissed him like that and then yelled at him to stay away from her and refused to even listen to his apology? He shouldn't have grabbed her in the pool or kissed her so impulsively, but he couldn't remember when anything had felt so right.

He should just leave. He had no idea why Kris had even invited him here. After his run yesterday, he'd steeled himself to ask she get dressed so they could talk and then knocked on her door again. She hadn't answered. He'd gone to the restaurant at one to meet her and she hadn't showed. Trying her door a few more times, he was pretty certain she'd disappeared, or was trying to ditch him. Who knew? She seemed unstable, at best.

He glared at the blizzard pummeling the windows of the resort. He probably couldn't leave even if he wanted to.

He wanted to find Quill Chadwick, or one of the other

Chadwicks, and see what they knew. Last night, he'd stayed away from the large gathering. He didn't want to ruin their pre-Christmas party and the weddings showing up as the illegitimate son, especially when he didn't know if that was even true.

Illegitimate. He hated that word. He wasn't some unwanted loser. He was an accomplished specialist and well-loved by his mom, their church group and neighbors, and many of his own friends. There were also numerous women chasing him. He frowned. Except for Ashley Casey. What was her deal anyway? How could she kiss him as if he were her long-lost love then rudely tell him to stay away from her as if he'd broken her heart?

He looked in the mirror and scrubbed at his beard. He'd studied some pictures of the Chadwick men online and he definitely saw the resemblance, especially the blue eyes. He straightened his shoulders and resolved to at least try to find one of the Chadwick men. Quill would be preferable—then he could ask what was going on with Kris—but he wouldn't mind talking to any of them. He'd ask them to keep his identity quiet until after Christmas so as not to upset the brides, but maybe he'd at least get an ally and friend out of the deal. A brother sounded even better. A brother. The idea made him happier than he'd been since Ashley had shoved him away in the pool.

He'd wanted to find out the truth before he hurt his mom, but he was going crazy. He needed answers. He tried her cell, but the call went to voice mail. He didn't leave one. That was strange. Unless she was rafting a river or scuba diving or some other crazy adventure, she always answered his calls.

Exiting his room, he walked toward the elevator. The stairwell door burst open and a blonde woman rushed out. She met his gaze and stopped in her tracks.

"Ashley?"

She was in a fitted white button-down shirt and blue pencil skirt. Her face was tear-stained and her blue eyes weren't done crying yet. She met his gaze for one heart-stopping moment, and he thought there might be a chance he could help her with whatever was wrong.

She stifled back a sob, mumbled, "Excuse me," and hurried around him.

Chase should just let her go, but apparently he was anxious for more punishment at her lovely hands. He was also very concerned about her.

She stopped outside a suite door at the very end of the hall and fumbled to pull her key card out. Chase approached her, stopped next to her, and gently touched her hand. "Are you okay?"

She turned to him and shocked him completely when her face crumpled, she cried out, "No," and then she fell against him.

Chase had no problem holding her close. Her tears fell unchecked for half a minute. At first, he was simply grateful she'd let him hold her, but then he started to grow concerned.

"Did someone hurt you?" he asked against her hair.

She looked up at him, her lovely blue eyes so bright and beautiful. "No."

"Oh, good." Relief rushed through him. "I didn't want to have to kill some man at Christmastime."

Her eyes widened in shock and she sputtered out a laugh. He chuckled too and then they were laughing together and he liked it, a lot. This was much better than her storming away from him at the pool, but not nearly as good as her kissing him.

A tense feeling rose between them as if she was thinking about that kiss too. She glanced up and her lips were soft and appealing. He found himself leaning down.

She pulled back, away from his touch. "Could you kill someone?" she asked, staring at him with a mixture of awe and wariness.

His eyes widened and he admitted, "My mom didn't believe in handouts. Nobody had given her any. So I went the Army route and became a dermatologist that way. So yeah, I've been trained how to kill somebody who dares to hurt a beautiful woman."

She gave him a flash of a smile. "I didn't realize the Army needed dermatologists."

"Even the toughest men can get a skin rash." He winked. The truth was he'd seen every condition in his years with the military. He'd almost lost two men to melanoma. A healthy twenty-two- and twenty-four-year-old respectively. Neither of them had even thought they were at risk because of their age, but luckily had been referred to him by a family practitioner concerned about a mole growing.

She stared at her door instead of at him and much more calmly pulled out her key. "I'm sorry about the bawling session." She waved her hand. "I didn't mean to break down on you."

"I'm glad I was here." He smiled, hoping she'd open up to him, but she studied the door. She apparently didn't want him here. He wondered again what he could have done to upset her so much this morning.

"Is there anything I can do to help?" He wanted to stop her before she went in that door and left him again.

She shook her head but at least she turned to face him again. "Unless you can stop the snow and the wind." She gave him a weak smile.

"Is it messing with your weddings?"

She nodded. "I think we're going to have to postpone at least

Iris and Devon's, if not Cruz and Meredith's." Her shoulders sagged.
"They have many friends out of the valley. Even the people in the
valley, the brides and grooms and most of their family will have a
near-impossible time getting here unless the storm lets up. They
might make it on snowmobiles, but it would be a nightmare. I'm not
willing to risk somebody getting lost or hurt, or ruining a wedding
dress." She glanced away. "I'm sorry. You probably think I'm such a
wimp. It's not just me I'm upset about. I mean, I am upset because
everything was planned to a T and it was going to be incredible, but
I'll be fine. It's Iris, Meredith, and Hope that I'm sad for."

"That's tough for a bride to plan her dream wedding and have
it taken away."

Her eyes widened and something flashed in them. "Yeah,
it is."

"Did that happen to you?" he asked.

She scanned her card across the door and it beeped and lit
green. Pushing on the handle, she shoved it open. "Thanks," she
muttered, hurrying through and then slamming it closed.

"Thanks for what?" he wondered aloud. He headed toward
the elevator again. He couldn't seem to win with her. It was a
mystery why he cared so much, but he couldn't stop himself. He
cared. He wanted to get to know her. Most of all, he wanted to
hold and kiss her again.

He went down the elevator, stewing on the weird conversation. At the front desk, there was a dark-haired girl popping her
gum. "Hi," he said. "I'm wondering if any of the Chadwick
family is here?"

"Nope," she said. "They're all warm and cozy in their beautiful houses during this vicious snowstorm. It's just the peons
like me that are stuck here running this huge resort and having

to sleep in a cot in the breakroom because all the suites are full. Luckily, the extra chefs and staff they brought in for the wedding stayed the night and have their own suites, but Raoul, the funny maître d' who is working into assistant manager too, also told me he hopes I'll work extra hours as a busser at the restaurants or a housekeeper. What a nightmare! I don't want to scrub poop off toilets!"

"Oh." He had no clue how to respond to her.

"I'm sorry. I'm so sorry." Her lower lip trembled. "Cat and Iris are the best bosses and I just love Grams and Chelsea. She used to work front desk with me, but she married that hot Aster and her little boy Dax is like my favorite. It's not like any of us knew the storm would get this bad last night and we'd all be stuck here. I'm super sad and totally freaked out that I might not get home for Christmas. It's my last Christmas, ever ..." She sniffled and Chase wondered what he was doing to make women cry today. "Cause, like, I'm going to college next year and this is it and my little sister is going to cry if I miss Christmas morning."

Chase gave her his reassuring doctor look, something he'd actually practiced for when he had to share bad news. "I'm sure you'll get home for Christmas. It's only the twenty-first."

She nodded and wiped at her face. "Sorry. Please don't tell anybody I got all unprofessional and stuff."

Chase lifted a hand. "It's between us."

Her pale blue eyes lit up and she slowly looked him over. "You're super hot for an old guy. I'm Daisy. I have a break at five if you want to, you know, like eat dinner together and ... other stuff."

Chase backed up. "No. No, thank you." He tried to soften his tone when her eyes got full of tears again. "I'm definitely too old for you."

Before she could say anything else, he speed-walked away. He went to explore the rest of the massive resort. The entire Chadwick family had been here last night along with a huge crowd, probably most of the little town. Now they were all tucked away in their houses or cabins weathering the storm. He walked to the massive windows overlooking the lake. He couldn't see much past the circle of outdoor light with huge white flakes swirling and smacking into the windows. Piles of snow covered the large deck.

He was stuck here in this massive resort until this storm cleared, Kris had disappeared, none of the Chadwicks were around, and now he needed to avoid that front desk girl. If only he could find Ashley and spend more time with her. He doubted it would go well with the animosity Ashley seemed to have for him. It seemed he wasn't going to meet his family until this storm passed, if the Chadwicks even were his family. Even worse, the woman he wanted to be interested in him definitely wasn't.

He walked to a quiet alcove and called his mom. He didn't want to upset her, but he needed some answers. The phone rang once and then her upbeat voice, "Handsome Rob!" It was a joke between them from the movie *The Italian Job*.

"Hi, Mom. How's ...?"

"Costa Rica? It's incredible. How's ...?"

"Mystical Lake? A blizzard."

"Oh, my. Are you all right?"

"Yeah. I'm in the huge resort. No worries. I'm safe and I'm sure they have plenty of food and stuff. Hey ..."

How did he ask her, over the phone, about his father that she'd never told him about?

"Hey, love. Ned and I are just getting clipped into a zipline. It's so gorgeous you wouldn't believe it. Flying over the jungle like I'm Tarzan. Ned's planned a huge day for us. I want to hear everything about you when I can sit down and focus. Can I call you tomorrow?"

"Oh, sure." It was a letdown and a relief. He wanted to know about his family, but he didn't want to hurt her. There was a distinct possibility the Chadwicks wouldn't want him around anyway, and his mom might put him off or refuse to tell him and he'd upset her for nothing. "Love you."

"I love you, sweetheart. Always praying for you. Mwah!"

The line went dead. He missed his mom and wished he'd gotten some answers, but he did love that she was off adventuring with Ned. Good for her.

He continued exploring the resort. It was pretty quiet besides some staff rushing around looking harried. He asked a couple of them if he could help, but they all smiled, reassured him everything was under control, and asked what they could do for him. Impressive staff. If Daisy hadn't broken down on him, he'd think they were fully staffed and prepared for this kind of emergency.

He wondered if most of the guests were just hunkering down in their suites hoping the storm would pass. Luckily, he found a group playing basketball in one of the indoor courts. He watched them play until a break when they immediately asked him to join in. He rushed to his room and changed. He got a great game and sweat in and made some new friends, a group of buddies from Idaho here with their wives.

After lunch, the wives joined in and Chase played pickle ball with all of them for a couple hours. The women talked the men, him included, into doing spa treatments because they couldn't think of anything else to do to pass the time besides Christmas movies in the main area. The spa treatments were relaxing. He didn't even mind the facial or pedicure, which were basically extended massages. The spa staff was limited, but none of his new friends minded waiting as they chatted or hung out in the steam rooms or therapy pools in between treatments. Sadly, no one at this resort had anything to kill but time. His mind was still stirring about Ashley and the Chadwicks, but at least he was passing the time.

His friends said goodbye to shower and go to dinner with their wives. They invited him, but he declined. It was one thing to be active with a bunch of happily married couples close to his age. It was quite another to sit at dinner as the odd man out.

He was again reminded that he was here alone. His desperation to find his father and maybe some siblings had gotten him here, but he was regretting it big-time. But if he hadn't come, he'd probably be stewing about whatever information he'd missed from Kris at his house in Missoula or one of his friends' houses. At least here he had the long shot of somehow getting Ashley to talk to him again.

He went back to his suite, showered, and dressed in a pale blue button-down shirt and black pants for dinner. He wanted to have dinner with Ashley. He wanted to know why she seemed drawn to him one minute and as if she wanted to punch him the next. He paced his room and watched the snow swirl, then he got all kinds of brave. Pushing into the hall, he stormed to Ashley's room and rapped on the door.

Twenty long seconds passed. He knew because he counted. He about gave up, but then the door swung softly open. Ashley stood there looking absolutely gorgeous in a soft-looking pale blue dress that highlighted her figure and looked amazing with her blonde hair and blue eyes.

"Hey," he said.

She looked him up and down. "We match."

He smiled and spread his hands. "I think that's an omen."

She tilted her head and her shiny curls spilled across her firm arm. "An omen for what?"

"That we should go to dinner together. Seeing as how we match and all."

She studied him for half a beat. He was terrified she was going to tell him to stay away from her, or slam the door in his face, but she simply said, "Okay."

Relief and excitement rushed through Chase. She was willingly going to spend time with him. He offered his elbow.

"One moment," she murmured.

"Of course."

She disappeared into the room and the door swung shut. Chase stood there, shifting nervously from foot to foot and hoping that door would reopen. She might be in there laughing at him or trying to figure out how many times she had to gently or not so gently tell him where to go before he finally got the message. When enough time passed that he was afraid she wasn't coming, the door finally opened and she walked out. She smelled like a tropical vacation and she looked even better.

"Sorry." She tucked a strand of hair back over her shoulder. "I wasn't quite ready."

"You look beautiful," he said.

She ducked her head slightly. "Thank you."

He offered his elbow again and she slid her hand into the crook of it. He felt like he was the king of the world as her hand wrapped around his bicep and they walked to the elevator.

Neither of them said anything as they rode down, nervous excitement playing between them. He'd heard about "sparks" between a man and a woman, but he had never felt them before. Could he convince her they should be dating? First, he had to get to the bottom of why she'd angrily stormed off this morning. He had a feeling it wasn't the best thing to bring up as dinner conversation.

They went to the steakhouse. It was busy, but a friendly maître d', Raoul, flirted with Ashley, told Chase he was a lucky man, and snuck them into a "romantic" back table for two.

Ashley didn't appear as happy about the romantic table as Chase was, though she thanked Raoul. Chase palmed him a ten and the friendly man went away grinning.

The waiter, Grayson, came quickly, took their drink orders, made recommendations, and was gone again. Silence fell between them. Chase didn't know her well, not really at all, but they'd kissed. Was that only this morning? There was something incredible between them, and at this point he couldn't make any progress finding information about his father, brothers, or sister. He'd much rather focus on Ashley than keep stressing about what may or may not be true.

He scrambled for something to say and finally settled on, "So how was your day ... after I saw you in the hallway?"

She gave him a blip of a smile and admitted, "Tough and boring."

"Tell me about that."

"Tough trying to decide what to do about the weddings and boring because there's not a lot I can do. I tried to help in the kitchens or with cleaning, but the staff all claimed they were fine and gently pushed me away. I hate not having anything to do."

He smiled, completely understanding and relating to that.

Also, he really liked that she was willing to offer to help. The situation must not have been as desperate as the dramatic front desk girl had made it sound. The resort seemed to be humming happily along with guests and staff all smiling like being snowed in was a grand adventure. He'd been bored earlier, but it wasn't a bad spot to get caught in a blizzard. There was plenty to do in the gorgeous resort, and Ashley was here. If he could talk her into spending every minute with him, he wouldn't mind the forced confinement at all.

The waiter brought their drinks and then took their orders. After he left, Chase asked, "So what is the plan with the weddings?"

She shook her head. "The storm isn't forecast to settle until the twenty-third." She frowned. "But the storm wasn't supposed to be this vicious of a blizzard either. I swear, if I failed at my job as much as the weather man ..." She trailed off and looked guiltily at him.

Chase laughed. Besides her telling him off, he got the sense she was a positive, kind person. It was funny to hear her cussing some unknown weather man.

"Anyway, after talking with each of the couples numerous times today, I'm pretty sure everyone is okay with doing multiple weddings on the twenty-third. We'll still have the big party on the twenty fourth with everyone at the resort and from town. If the storm doesn't clear until then, that will be our wedding day."

"More work for you?" he guessed.

She shrugged. "At least it gives me something to do while we wait out this snowstorm."

"You could hang out with me." She looked dubious, so he rushed to say something that she might want to do with him. "I got a facial, a massage, a pedicure, and a manicure today."

"You did not."

"Did too."

She stared strangely at him. "Why?"

He shrugged his shoulders. "Something to do, and it could be considered research. I'm thinking of adding a couple estheticians to my office."

She looked at him as if she wasn't certain if she bought his excuse. He held out his hand to her. "Look how baby soft it is."

She ran her fingertips along the back of his hand, making him tremble, which was awkward and amazing at the same time. Before she could withdraw her hand, he turned his palm over and aligned it with hers.

"Baby soft?" he asked, gazing into her blue eyes.

The tension ramped up between them. He wanted to grab her and pull her in for a long, drawn-out kiss. She ran her palm along his and he may or may not have let out a very un-manly moan.

She smiled slightly and admitted, "Baby soft." She didn't withdraw her hand. He was happy and content right now, but would it continue? This woman was very touch and go.

"Also, the facial. My cheeks are soft as a baby's bum." He leaned in closer. "Do you want to touch them?"

"Your cheeks can't be soft. They're covered in hair."

He grinned, but even the teasing didn't dispel the fireworks arcing between them. "All that goop the lady put on them had to condition the hair of my beard. Try it out and let me know."

She smiled and shook her head, but she lifted her free hand and ran it over the side of his cheek, along his jaw, and then down to his neck. He shivered, in an incredibly good way.

"Your fingers are soft as a baby's too," he said.

"Any other treatments that made you soft as a baby?"

They studied each other. He wanted to tell her she could touch his back—the massage therapist had used a mixture of almond and coconut oil that may have softened his skin—but he thought she would balk at that. "I got a pedicure," he admitted.

She laughed and pulled her hands back. "I am not touching your feet to see how soft they are."

He smiled, feeling withdrawal from her hands not touching him. "Your loss."

The waiter brought their salads and they started eating. Chase asked about her career and how she got into wedding planning. Her steak pasta and his ribs and veggies were delivered and they both delved into them as they talked.

She asked about the army and his schooling. They talked a little bit about their families. The conversation was easy and they made it comfortably to chocolate devotion dessert before she tilted her head and asked, "And why are you here? For the weddings or Christmas or because your mom is in South America or are you here *with* someone?" She rattled off all these questions quickly, but seemed focused on him being here with someone.

He suddenly felt awkward. Could he tell her about Kris luring him here and the crazy idea of finding his dad and that the Chadwicks might be his half-siblings? She stared at him as if his answer meant everything to her.

"Um, well ..." Chase always felt confident and comfortable, but he was neither right now. Maybe it wouldn't hurt to tell her what was going on, but he hadn't even told his own mother. "I don't know quite how to ... explain. I need to have a ... difficult discussion with someone before I should really talk about it." He shifted in his seat and took a quick shot of his water to give him a second to compose his thoughts. Was he making any sense or confusing her as much as he was confused? If only the dream of a father and siblings wasn't such a strong lure for him.

"It's okay." Ashley held up her hand as if to ward him off. "It's your business. Really, no stress if you don't want to tell me."

He felt relieved. His mom should call back tomorrow. He could talk to her and see if he could get to the bottom of his father mystery. Then when the storm cleared and he wasn't messing up somebody's wedding, he could talk to the Chadwicks. He wondered where Kris had disappeared to, but he was relieved not to deal with her. He'd texted and called a few times and gotten no response.

"Thank you," he told Ashley.

She abruptly stood, clutching her little hand purse thing and pulling out a hundred-dollar bill. "I've got to go. Lots of work to do. Let me just leave this for dinner." She dropped the hundred on the table and turned to go.

Chase stood, grabbed the money, and shoved it back into her little purse. "Keep your money. I've got dinner."

Why was she ditching him? She'd admitted earlier that she didn't have much to do.

"No." She glared up at him. "This wasn't a date. I can pay my share."

"It absolutely was a date," he insisted, offended. They'd finally relaxed, talked, even joked and touched his "baby soft" skin. What had he done now and why didn't she want to be on a date with him?

"Was not." She jutted out her chin.

"Was."

Grayson chose that moment to appear. Chase quickly pulled out a credit card and thrust it at the competent waiter. "Thank you, Grayson."

Ashley tried to pull the hundred out of her purse to hand it to the man, but the waiter was already walking away. She glared up at Chase. "I'll leave this for a tip."

"Not necessary," Chase asserted, pulling out a hundred from his own wallet and dropping it on the table.

"Argh," Ashley growled at him. "You're infuriating." She turned to march away, but turned back and lifted a hand as if she was royalty. "Thank you for dinner, Dr. Hamilton. Goodnight." Then she strode off without looking back.

So they were back to *Dr. Hamilton?* Every instinct screamed for Chase to rush after her, lift her off her feet, and kiss her. Instead, he stood rooted to the spot and watched her go.

Grayson reappeared with his card and a slip for him to sign. "Everything all right, sir?" Grayson asked. "With the lady?"

Chase shook his head and signed the slip. "She exited stage left."

"I'm sorry, sir. I thought things were going well."

"Me too, Grayson. Me too." He shook his head and then shook the man's hand, palming him the hundred that he'd plucked off the table.

"Thank you, sir."

"Dinner was great." He studied the young waiter. "Do you understand women, Grayson?"

The kid smiled and shook his head. "No, sir ... but they seem to understand us."

Chase chuckled. "Too true." He clapped him on the shoulder. "Thanks again. Goodnight."

"Goodnight, sir."

He walked slowly from the restaurant, watching snow swirl and plaster the large windows. For the past couple hours, he hadn't minded being stuck in this snowstorm because he'd been with Ashley. Right now, he wanted to escape these walls. What he really wanted was to bang on Ashley's door and figure out how she could be so hot and cold. Something about him not telling her why he was here. Was she suspicious? Did she think he looked like the Chadwicks and she was protecting them? He'd asked a few questions about the Chadwicks at dinner, but he didn't think he'd grilled her for info or anything.

He didn't know what to think, but the night had taken a very depressing turn. He headed to his room, hoping there would at least be a way to buy a Crusaders movie or Lord of the Rings. He could really use some fighting, battles, and destruction right now.

CHAPTER FOUR

Ashley could not believe Chase's nerve and her own short-term memory loss. He was here with that woman. He needed to have a "tough conversation with someone?" What did that mean? He'd dump that lady for Ashley? He had to be with a woman. No man—especially a tough ex-Army man—got a pedicure, manicure, and facial without a woman forcing him to. He'd spent all day with someone else and now wanted to touch and flirt with Ashley. Ugh!

Every time Chase saw Ashley, he flirted with her unabashedly. He'd taken her to dinner, acting for all the world as if he wanted to be with her, claiming it was a date and paying for it. Yet when she'd asked why he was here or if he was with someone, he couldn't explain, and when she gave him the out, he'd thanked her. Thanked her for cheating with him? She'd also seen him talking with Daisy from the front desk and the girl had propositioned him before Ashley could get away. He'd probably accepted! Ooh, she was so ticked at him she couldn't even sleep.

At five a.m., she was dressed and heading to the gym, glaring at the snow still hitting the windows. Would this storm ever blow itself out? She tried to reassure herself that things were going to work out fine with the weddings. Truthfully, it wasn't as if this gorgeous resort was a hard place to be snowed in. A million times better than her small apartment in Missoula. If only Chase wasn't here. If only she wasn't acting so crazy with him. But he deserved it. Was he with that woman who'd pulled him into her suite on the fourth floor? She wished she knew, but when she'd asked, he'd dodged, which made her think he definitely was. And for all she knew, the fourth-floor woman wasn't the only one.

She swept her card over the reader by the door and walked into the gym. Empty. Just the way she liked it. She was generally a people person, but when she worked out, she liked to go hard, get nice and sweaty, and not have anybody watching or interrupting.

She was doing inchworms across the open area of the gym when the door whooshed open. She paused with her hands and feet on the floor and her bum in the air, almost a downward dog position and tilted her head to gawk. Chase strode into the room, looking like he owned the space. That wasn't uncharacteristic. With his confidence, he owned whatever space he was in.

"Ashley?" He tilted his head as if to go upside down himself.

Ashley straightened, tugged her t-shirt down, and flipped her hair back over her shoulder. "Hey," she managed, catching a breath. Chase looked incredible in a t-shirt and shorts. How lame was that? It was only a t-shirt and shorts. His broad shoulders filled out the shirt nicely and the muscles revealed in his arms and legs were nothing to sneer at.

"Did you sleep well?" he asked conversationally, as if it wasn't five a.m., he wasn't with that woman, and Ashley hadn't stormed away from him last night.

"No. You?"

He smirked. "Not well, no. Did the storm keep you up?"

She folded her arms across her chest and raised an imperious eyebrow. "I don't think the storm was to blame."

He chuckled. "I'm with you." His gaze traveled slowly over her and he said in a deeper tone, "But what man could sleep picturing beauty such as yours?"

Her heart skipped a beat and she wanted to lose herself in his blue eyes. Instead, she forced herself to ignore the compliment and turned, searching for a machine close by. She found the seated row and quickly adjusted the weight and sat, grabbing the metal handles.

She heard his footsteps approach and couldn't resist looking up. He looked really tall with her sitting down. She automatically stood to shorten the discrepancy, but then she was right in his space. He smelled good. Who smelled good at five a.m.?

"Do you mind if I work out in here with you?" he asked. The way he was looking at her made her tremble, as if he remembered exactly how fabulous that kiss had been yesterday morning in the pool and he wanted to replicate it, right now. She wouldn't mind. Her heart picked up a beat and her stomach swooped as she remembered being in his arms.

She tried to snap herself out of the trance he put her in. *He's two-timing some other woman*, she reminded herself. *And flirting with seventeen-year-old front desk staff to boot.*

It wasn't as if she was going to let herself fall in love at Christmastime again. You'd think she'd learned her lesson after being engaged to seven too-flirtatious men close to Christmas, but no. She was thick in the head.

"It's a big gym," she said flippantly, pointing to a rack of hand weights. "Stay on your side."

"My side?" He arched an eyebrow and moved closer. His chest brushed her arm and her heart raced out of control. "What if I really want to use the machines? Say I need the seated row?" He was far too close and she could not catch a breath.

"We can, um ..." Her mind scrambled for some solution to keep him out of her space. "Switch sides. If you really want the machines, then I'll start with hand weights. Then we'll switch so you can use the hand weights. I'll set a timer." She was talking a mile per minute, obviously revealing how stirred up he made her.

She scurried around him and pulled out her phone. He turned to look at her with an amused expression, but there was also a hunger in his eyes that was making her far too warm. "Half an hour all right?"

Chase crossed the distance between them and she found herself leaning into a cable machine and panting for air. He rested one hand on the metal support above her head. "You're certain you don't want to lift together?"

Ashley's chest rose and fell quickly. She reached back and held on to the side of the machine so she didn't reach for him. He was so close and so attractive. "I lift alone."

He arched an eyebrow, giving her a smolder that both drew her in and infuriated her. He was such a womanizer and she had to be strong. His gaze trailed over her lips then met her eyes again. "Your loss."

It was definitely, definitely her loss, but she wasn't going to fall for a player. Not again and especially not at Christmastime. She had learned her lesson, no matter how irresistible this man was to her.

Dodging under his arm, she raced for the free weights, stopping to program a thirty-minute timer before shoving her phone back in her pocket and grabbing a pair of fifteen-pound dumbbells. She did her level best to ignore Chase, but there were mirrors on every wall. No matter where she looked, she could see him. The gym was several steps nicer and larger than any hotel gym she'd been in, but it wasn't massive.

The only sound was the weights clanking or dropping and their breathing. Every time he caught her eye, he gave her a lingering smile. Dang him all to heck. She lifted as hard as she had in months. Sweat was rolling down her face when the alarm sounded in the quiet gym. She quickly pulled her phone out and shut it off.

"Time to switch?" he asked from across the room.

"Yes."

She set the weights down and walked across the room, trying to avoid looking at him. He edged close and stopped right in front of her. Ashley's head arched back and she studied his handsome face.

"I didn't bring my phone," he said. "Would you mind turning some music on?" He gave her an incredible smile. "It's far too quiet in here. My mind has too much space to wander." His gaze wandered over her face and rested on her lips as he said that.

None of her ex-fiancés were as good at flirting as he was. He drew her in so fast she felt like she was falling off a cliff. "Oh, um ..." She licked her lips and tried to focus. "Music? Sure."

"Thanks," he said, giving her a knowing smirk. He knew exactly how effective his looks were.

She nodded and hurried around him before she did something stupid like grabbing him. Reaching the cable machine, she pulled out her phone, opened her music app, and found her running playlist. She pushed play and turned the volume up all the way. It sounded tinny and too quiet, but it was better than listening for each and every one of his exhales and wondering how sweet his breath would feel against her face. She imagined him leaning close, his arms trapping her in place against the cable machine in the best possible way. His breath would brush her lips and then his lips would brush hers ...

"No!" she cried out.

Chase spun, dropped the weights, and was halfway across the weight room before she realized she'd screamed out loud.

"Ashley?" He wasted no time getting to her side. She released her grip on the bar attached to the cable machine as Chase grasped her arms gently in his hands. "Are you okay?"

She stared into his blue eyes and wondered how she could explain. No, she was not okay, and though he didn't realize it, her messed up state of mind was all his fault. She bit her lip and shook her head. "Yes. I mean, no." She nodded. "I'm fine. I saw a ... spider."

"Oh." He stared at her as if he didn't want to step away or let her go, but thankfully he did both. "Where is it? I can kill it."

Ashley put a hand to her heart. Of course he'd be that man. The man who'd willingly kill spiders for her, even when she was lying to him about seeing one. "Thanks, but it's fine. It ran off when I screamed. Not like you. You ran *to* me when I screamed." She pressed her lips together. She needed to stop talking.

He gave her a devastatingly handsome smile. If she wasn't a sweaty mess—and a hot mess where he was concerned—she would've thrown herself into his arms. Instead, she turned back and grabbed the bar. He stayed by her side for a few drawn-out seconds as she used the bar for triceps pulldown. He finally seemed to give up on her talking to him more and returned to his side of the gym.

As she tried to avoid staring at him, used various machines, and listened to upbeat songs rotating from her playlist, she had an awful thought. She might need to switch careers. Being involved in so many couples' happiest day was distorting her vision of reality and making her think that love and marriage were possible for her. She'd tried to replicate the joy she saw in her clients over and over. She needed to face reality, but she couldn't see things clearly when faced with the most incredible man she'd ever met.

No. He couldn't be incredible because she was ninety percent certain he was a cheater.

The ten percent troubled her deeply.

What if Chase wasn't a womanizer and he could explain the interactions she'd seen with him and other women? Ashley didn't dare even ask him about it or let herself fantasize that he might be a good guy who was sincerely interested in her. She was damaged from too many failed relationships and horrified at the thought of falling for an appealing man near Christmas as she had before. She had to be smart about this.

She glanced at Chase as he did a lateral raise, the muscles in his shoulders and arms flexing so nicely her mouth went dry. Was she destined for unfulfilled romance in her life? Or was there a chance Chase was as incredible as he seemed and the perfect fit for her? Maybe he was the man who could make her believe in love again.

How pathetic was she? A wedding planner who didn't believe in love anymore. But who could blame her after her so many failed attempts?

His eyes lifted and focused on her. She felt hot all over.

The song changed to a slow beat and she instantly recognized, "Say You Won't Let Go," by James Arthur. Oh no! This song was on her wedding playlist, not her workout. What was going on?

Her heart raced and her eyes darted toward Chase. He set the weights down and slowly walked toward her. She couldn't tear her gaze from him. He sang along with the song, "I pulled you closer to my chest."

She thought her own chest was going to split with how fast her heart was racing.

He stepped in close and asked, "Do you want to dance?"

"Dance?" she asked, panting for breath. "Here? Now?"

He smiled. "Yes, please."

"I'm all sweaty and I can't ..."

His blue gaze held hers steadily. "Can't what?"

"Chase, don't do this to me," she begged.

His eyebrows rose slightly. "What am I doing to you?"

"Making me—"

The door to the gym swung open and she turned to see a twenty-something-year-old brunette in a tight tank top and short shorts strut in. "Hi, y'all," she waved happily. Her gaze zeroed in on Chase and she moistened her lips with her tongue.

"Hi." Ashley waved back and scurried away from Chase. She'd almost revealed to him that he was making her fall for him. That would've been very stupid of her to share. Maybe he wasn't a player like she feared, but he was incredibly handsome and appealing and women naturally went after him. That wasn't his fault. It was on Ashley that she'd been through too many failed relationships to want to go through it again. But there was something special about Chase. She couldn't deny it, but it made her want to run even faster.

Chase eventually went back to the free weights and the beautiful girl stayed right close to him, flirting unabashedly. Ashley tried to be objective about the one-sided conversation she heard. Chase didn't encourage the girl, and he did try to move several times, but she followed him like a shadow.

Ashley tried to concentrate on lifting, but she needed to get out of here before she exploded and did something stupid like telling the girl off for innocently flirting. Or worse, grabbing Chase and kissing him.

When Chase was in the middle of a seated bicep curl, she darted out the door and ran down the hallway to the stairs and up the five flights to her room. She made it inside. Had he chased her? She waited by the door for almost a minute. Nothing.

Deflated and frustrated, mostly with herself, she headed for the shower.

CHAPTER FIVE

Chase was doing curls one second and the next, the gym door banged closed and Ashley had disappeared. He wanted to run after her, but how low could one man let his pride dip? They'd been close for one moment and then she'd dodged him again.

The brunette who'd interrupted him and Ashley kept flirting unabashedly with him, no matter that he didn't encourage her. He tried to be nice but hurried through the end of his workout and retreated to his room. With nothing to do, he put on a swimsuit and did laps like yesterday. The pool was soothing, but it allowed his mind to wander for too long. Ashley was at the forefront of his thoughts. He still wanted to know about the Chadwicks and if he was their unwanted brother, but none of them were around, Kris had disappeared, and his mom wasn't calling him back. He felt strangely distanced from any worries besides how to drop his pride completely and beg Ashely to talk to him. Ashley's beautiful face and clever comments played through his mind over and over as he swam.

He ate a late breakfast and found his basketball friends. Playing some intense games with them killed a few hours, but then they had to go shower and spend time with their wives. He didn't know what to do with himself. He wandered through the massive resort, running into the front desk girl, Daisy, and the brunette from the gym, whose name he couldn't remember.

To his disappointment, he didn't spot Ashley anywhere.

The storm was incredible and relentless. If Ashley was interested in him, he'd think he was trapped in the most beautiful Hallmark Christmas movie set he'd ever seen. His mom used to make him watch those on occasion. They were cheesy and he liked to tease his mom about them, but the settings were pretty and he secretly didn't mind the romance.

Everyone at the resort was friendly and no one seemed overly concerned about the storm, but Chase was starting to feel as if they were all in a beautiful, icy prison. Without any time with Ashely, he was more than ready to escape.

At least he wasn't completely consumed worrying if he was a Chadwick. There was nothing he could do about that until the storm passed and the Chadwicks came to the resort again. Right now, Ashley was all he could think about.

Checking his phone, he was shocked he hadn't missed a call from his mom, or at least a text with pictures from her and Ned's latest adventure. She was normally very involved in Chase's life. The past six weeks, she'd checked in most days with phone or video chats and sent pictures.

He tried her again, but it rang and rang and then went to voicemail. He didn't leave one. She'd get back to him. She must be busy with her adventuring, and Ned. He smiled. At least his mom had romance in her life with a great person, even if Chase didn't.

His wandering led him back to the main area. The resort staff had set up a large movie screen and dimmed the lights. With the storm keeping the sky outside pretty dark, *The Santa Clause* was easily visible. The staff had moved couches and comfortable chairs into place and there was a decent crowd watching the movie. The smell of popcorn and cocoa was soothing, reminding him of Christmas with his mom. This particular movie made him flash back to when he'd first seen it as a young child. He'd decided halfway through the film that was why his dad wasn't around—his father was obviously Santa Claus. He smiled at the memory. Though he'd been sad when he realized his theory wasn't true, his mom had made that and every Christmas a magical, fun, and spiritual time together.

He strolled behind the crowd, not sure if he wanted to stay but not sure what else to do. This snow needed to ease up so he could get outside and burn off more energy. He was in a sad state of mind when lifting, swimming, and basketball weren't enough to keep him calm. Maybe it had been a mistake to come to Mystical Lake. He wouldn't have connected with Ashley again if he hadn't come, but apparently she didn't want to be around him and that made him pretty miserable.

He approached a long table next to the viewing area set up with buttered popcorn and a hot cocoa bar with a variety of toppings. Maybe he'd at least get some hot cocoa and popcorn, take it back to his suite, and watch another Crusaders movie. Alone. It was very telling that he'd rather watch action and adventure by himself than Christmas shows at Christmastime with a crowd. His mom would say he needed to find some Christmas spirit, but it wasn't fun to be in a crowd by himself.

He fixed himself a cocoa, grabbed a bag of popcorn, told the staff thank you, turned, and immediately spotted Ashley. If a beam of light would've come from the heavens at that moment and told him, *This is the right one, go for it*, he wouldn't have been surprised.

She was sitting on a loveseat with no one next to her. Apprehension had his stomach hopping. She was so intently focused on the movie. It was like she'd seen him but didn't want to acknowledge him. Was she avoiding his gaze because she didn't want him to come sit by her?

He was nervous and keyed up, but he couldn't reject any opportunity to spend time with her. Maybe this time, she wouldn't ditch him. He clung to his treats and slowly approached her. She didn't have any popcorn, only a Styrofoam cup of cocoa in her hands. He stopped right next to her and thankfully she glanced up. If she had ignored him, he may have done something un-manly like crying.

"Is this seat taken?"

She stared up at him. Her throat bobbed as she swallowed, but thankfully she said quietly, "No."

Chase wanted to cheer, but he'd probably dump his popcorn and upset the movie watchers. He was already standing in somebody's way, but luckily they were too nice to yell "down in front"—or middle, since Ashley's loveseat was about halfway from the front.

He eased onto the loveseat right next to her. Setting his cocoa on the floor, he offered the popcorn to her.

"Thanks," she mumbled, taking a small handful.

He ate some popcorn, drank some of the salty caramel hot cocoa, and tried to focus on the movie. He failed. Ashley was right here. She looked good in a long white sweater and tight black jeans, her blonde hair tousled in soft curls. She smelled good, like she should be on a beach, and he wondered if she had a secret longing for a tropical Christmas. If she did, he would happily fly them both to Costa Rica so she could meet his mom and Ned before Chase proposed.

The room was suddenly sweltering hot. He was insane, but now he couldn't get the image of her and him on a beach out of his mind—or even better, her walking down the aisle to him. He wasn't usually a fanciful dreamer, but he could definitely dream about her. Her arm brushed against the length of his as she reached for more popcorn and he thought he might combust.

In what he hoped was a casual tone, he asked, "Whose idea was the movie?"

"Mine," she admitted.

"I wondered," he said in a hushed tone. He smiled and she returned it. "That party planning instinct?"

"For sure," she whispered back, easing in a little closer so he could hear her. He'd take any closeness for any reason. "Iris and Cat are stressing not being here with their guests to weather the storm, so I've planned a few activities for this afternoon and evening to reassure them everyone is having a good time. Hopefully the storm dies by tomorrow for the weddings." She cast a worried glance at the stormy sky visible through the floor to ceiling windows behind them.

"What other activities do you have planned?" he asked. Ashley knew the Chadwicks well. He wished he was comfortable enough to ask for an introduction after the weddings. The idea of a father, little sister, and a whole passel of brothers was exciting to say the least, but he kept trying not to let his hopes get too high.

"You missed the earlier activities. The staff taught guests

how to fold towels and napkins into impressive shapes. There was also a sushi-making demonstration and a tour of the kitchens. Plus a belly-flop competition in the pool."

"Shoot. I could've won that one." He was most likely in the gym playing basketball through all of that.

She smiled.

"What else do you have planned?"

"After the movie, they're doing a huge buffet dinner, free to everyone. Then we've got a couple of fun games—family feud and the newlywed game—then a dance-off later tonight."

"Sounds like a lot of fun. Can I help with anything?" Would she dance with him? She hadn't in the gym earlier, but maybe he'd made that awkward. They'd both been sweaty and the timing had probably been off.

She tilted her head and studied him. Suddenly he wanted nothing more than to touch one of those silky blonde curls. He dug his fingernails into his palms to stop himself from reaching out.

"If I need help, I'll let you know," she said.

He didn't think she would, but he couldn't keep begging for her attention and getting rejected. At least they were sitting here comfortably right now. He offered her the popcorn.

She shook her head. "No, thanks."

He set the popcorn next to his half-empty hot cocoa and edged closer to her. Their arms brushed and she looked up at him. He slid his hand against hers and intertwined their fingers. She let out the cutest little gasp, but she didn't pull her hand away, so he counted it as a huge win. Her gaze locked with his. Was that an invitation he read there? He leaned closer, thinking he could definitely make it an invitation. That kiss in the pool was never far from his mind.

Suddenly people were clapping and then the lights turned brighter. She pulled back and stated the obvious with a little frown that made him very happy. "The movie's over."

"Yeah, it is." He nodded. It was probably good the movie had ended or he would've kissed her again. He wanted to, but he wanted it to be in private and he wanted to know that she wanted it. How could he get to the bottom of why she was so up and down with him?

"I need to go." She stood abruptly.

He stood also. "Okay. Let me know if you need help. I'll just be ... hanging out here."

"Thanks." She rushed off.

He got a plate from the buffet and sat and ate with a friendly family from southern California. He thought the teenagers would be more upset that they were stuck inside, but they were both excited about the storm and could hardly wait to play in the snow as soon as it stopped coming down so hard. He kept one eye on Ashley. She didn't stop to eat anything, instead hurrying around talking to people and getting things ready for the games.

The first game, Family Feud, started as everyone was filling their plates with a myriad of desserts. Most people took their dessert and specialty drinks over to the couches and chairs that had been set up for the movie to watch the impromptu game show. The show was fun. Raoul, the maître d' from the steak house, was the show host and he did a great job, teasing with everyone and flirting with the older ladies, making them laugh and blush.

Chase kept one eye on the show and one on Ashley. She was still busy running around, but as the show was winding down, she stood at the back of the room looking nervous and uncertain. That didn't seem characteristic of her. She had seemed in her element setting everything up.

He met her gaze and mouthed, *You okay?*

She bit her lip, folded her arms across her chest, and finally mouthed back, *I need help.*

He grinned. She needed him. Standing quickly, he hurried down the aisle and to her side. A couple of his basketball buddies whispered loudly, "Chase," as he walked past. He lifted a hand in greeting, but he couldn't stop. Ashley needed him.

She leaned back to meet his gaze and he said in a false western tone, "How can I be of service, little lady?"

She smiled, but she still looked stressed. "For the newlywed game, we need four couples to participate."

He nodded his encouragement.

"A couple that are dating, a couple that are newlyweds, a couple that have been married twenty years, and a couple that have been married fifty years."

"That should make it fun."

"Yes, but ..." She glanced at Raoul and the feuding families. "We can't find a dating couple." She looked at him and then away again.

Chase felt a blip of confusion but then it hit him. "You and I can be the dating couple." Joy rushed through him. This might be the breakthrough he needed.

"We aren't actually dating," she reminded him.

He took her hand in his. It was cold. He rubbed it gently between both of his. "I know, but I want to be dating you. That should count for something."

She stared up at him, bit at her lip again, and then said quickly, "You aren't dating anyone else?"

"Not seriously."

"What does that mean?" She pulled her hand back.

He pushed a hand at his hair. "I go on dates, but I'm not in a serious relationship." He lowered his voice. "But if you were interested, I would love to talk about a serious relationship with you."

Her blue eyes looked conflicted. Applause sounded as the game show finished. Would she take him seriously? They stared at each other, neither saying anything.

The young girl from the front desk tapped Ashley's arm. "They're ready for you, Miss Casey." She turned to Chase. "Oh, hey-a, handsome. It's Daisy, remember? That offer to hang out is still on the table. I've been working loads of hours, so I've got *all* night off after this." She gave him a lewd wink.

Chase's neck felt hot and he backed away. "Sorry, but ..."

Ashley grabbed his arm. "Dr. Hamilton is with me," she said primly, giving the girl a stern look.

"Oh! Shoot. My bad. Good job, Miss Casey. He is f-i-n-e, fine."

"Thank you, Daisy," Ashley gritted out, then tugged Chase toward the front of the room.

He took her hand in his and matched her frenzied pace. He was able to lean down and whisper, "Thank you for saving me."

She glared up at him. "Did you want to be saved?"

"Yes." He met her challenging gaze with one of his own. "Do you want to date me?"

Ashley blew out a breath and Raoul announced, "And our couples are all here! Let's introduce them."

"Chase!" his basketball friends all screamed for him as the rest of the crowd clapped politely.

Chase lifted a hand to wave, trying to smile and act happy, but Ashley was messing with his head. All he wanted was to get her alone and talk for hours. He had to focus on helping her through this game show, but tonight he was determined to get some answers from her.

He had lots of questions. Why did she keep ditching him? Would she kiss him again? Most importantly—would she date him, seriously date him? He'd never felt like this about any woman. Forget his pride. He was pursuing Ashley with everything he had.

CHAPTER SIX

Ashley half-listened to Raoul and the crowd, some of the men cheering raucously for Chase. She didn't know he had friends here at the resort. Not of the male variety, anyway. She didn't know near enough about him. She wanted to get him alone and ask a lot of questions. Right now, she couldn't think what questions. All she could think about was Chase's hand around hers and the intent way he'd looked at her and asked if she wanted to date him. The answer would be a screaming yes... if she knew he wouldn't cheat on her and she could break her pattern of engaged by Christmas, planning a spring wedding, and ditching the groom, sometimes on the wedding day.

Sadly, she was falling in love at Christmas once again, and the red flags that she'd missed before were all there with Chase. Women flocked to him, he was extremely handsome, and he was a natural flirt. She frowned. *Was* he a natural flirt? She'd actually only heard him flirt with her. He hadn't encouraged the front desk girl or the gorgeous brunette from the gym, even though

Ashley had seen both of them blatantly flirting with him. Even the woman who'd pulled him into her room. He hadn't said anything flirtatious back to her, but he'd walked in that room on his own two feet.

Dang, she was confused.

"I think you're supposed to be smiling as they introduce us," Chase whispered into her ear, his warm breath doing a number on her sensitive skin.

Ashley was startled back to reality. Chase lifted their joined hands to wave to the crowd as Raoul cried out, "And our beautiful dating couple. Wow, these two look good together, don't they?"

"Chase! Chase! Chase!" his friends hollered.

Ashley's stomach swooped. She wished this wasn't a farce and that scared her. Her family and friends would flip out if she fell in love during the holidays once again. Her mom would definitely tell her off and have a conniption fit. But as she looked at Chase ... Would they really make a fuss? Or would they be thrilled she'd found someone as incredible as Chase?

Was eighth time the charm?

"Thanks," Chase replied smoothly for them.

"We don't know nearly enough about our dating couple. Ashley, can you share the dirt on you two?"

Ashley forced a bright smiled and said, "We don't want to tell you too much or it might ruin the suspense of the game questions."

The crowd laughed, but a few booed at her attempt to distract them.

"All right, all right." Raoul put up his hands and winked. "At least allow me to introduce our beautiful wedding coordinator, Ashley Casey, and her boyfriend ..."

The word boyfriend made Ashley's heart race. After all her failed attempts at dating and being engaged, she'd think it was a panic attack, but with Chase at her side, her hand in his, it was a good kind of race.

"Chase Hamilton," Chase said, waving his free hand and gifting the crowd with his charming smile. Several women *ahh*ed.

"Where are you from, Chase?" Raoul asked.

"Missoula, just like Ashley."

"And what do you do in Missoula, my friend?"

"I'm a dermatologist."

"Ooh." Raoul whistled and the crowd applauded. "So our handsome boyfriend is also a doctor. Good choice, Miss Casey, very good indeed."

Ashley kept smiling as some of the women in the crowd eyed Chase like he was a large slice of strawberry cheesecake and they were officially done with their diets. Her hand tightened around his and she cuddled in closer and rested her head against his shoulder. "Thank you," she said to Raoul. "I'll fight to keep him." She gave the brunette from the gym this morning a significant look. The woman returned it and then some, her eyes narrowing and her lips thinning. She was obviously ready for battle.

Chase released Ashley's hand and wrapped his arm snugly around her back, splaying his palm around her hip and warming her clear through. "She doesn't have to fight. She's already won my heart," he said.

The crowd cheered, loving that. After a few seconds, Raoul waved his hands to calm them down. "I'm sure we'll hear more sugary sweetness from our loving doc soon."

Ashley didn't know how to react to the words "loving doc." Chase wasn't in love with her. He was only helping her out. Had she gotten them into a mess because she wanted the show to go well?

Raoul gave instructions and seated them in hard chairs that had been placed back to back. He handed them pads of paper and pens to answer the questions. Ashley wondered how much of Chase's sweet line was for the crowd. He'd asked her if she'd date him. Did she really dare take that leap again?

She only half paid attention as Raoul chatted and teased and the questions began. They weren't doing the traditional newlywed game where the couples were split up and each answered questions separately. They would both answer the question, then Raoul would read their answers and of course give them a hard time. Daisy from the front desk was keeping score. Even though she'd approved it, Ashley couldn't remember what the prize for winning was. She doubted they'd win anyway.

"And every time you get an answer right, we get to see a kiss," Raoul announced happily.

The crowd roared their approval.

Ashley's stomach dropped and then lifted and then swirled as if she was a human roller coaster. What on earth? Raoul had added that in without her approval. She had to kiss Chase if they got the answers right? In front of this crowd? She was terrified to commit to any man, but nothing had felt as good as kissing Chase. Even if she couldn't commit, she could kiss the dickens out of him when they got an answer right and it wouldn't mean they were together. Wait a minute. That would mean she was playing him. She didn't feel right about that.

She suddenly noticed the other couples writing their answers. She hadn't even heard the question. Oh my. She glanced around and caught Daisy's eye and mouthed. *What was the question?*

Daisy smiled and then giggled. She hurried to whisper in Ashley's ear, but Raoul noticed. "What's wrong here, pretty girls?"

"Ashley didn't hear the question," Daisy announced loudly.

Raoul chuckled. "Too busy contemplating those kisses when you get the answer right?"

"Yes," she admitted before she could stop herself.

The crowd hooted at that. Luckily, she couldn't see how Chase responded, but he reached back and brushed the side of her arm with his hand and whispered, "I'm with you."

Ashley's heart raced out of control.

Raoul could hardly contain his laughter. He'd obviously heard Chase. "The first question is: Where was your first kiss and who initiated it?"

Oh my, oh my, oh my! She should've known these questions would be invasive. Why had she let Raoul be in charge of the games? He'd told her he found some fun, safe questions on the Internet and she'd trusted him. She should've at least vetted the questions, but she hadn't known she'd be participating with none other than Chase Hamilton. She forced her shaking fingers to grip the pencil tightly and somehow managed to write out her answer.

Raoul started with the older couple and worked his way down. Ashley's stomach tumbled as she half-listened to the funny answers, the couples giving each other a hard time, the crowd laughing or cheering, and Raoul eating it up and making it worse. Finally, he said, "First kiss for our dating couple?"

He took Ashley's paper and read aloud. "'Mystical Lake Resort swimming pool.' Whoo-ee! Spicy kiss, my friend!" The crowd laughed and cheered. "'Chase initiated it.'" He nodded. "That makes sense. He's a man's man. Of course he'd initiate."

He winked at Ashley and then took Chase's paper. "'Mystical Lake Resort swimming pool. I initiated it.' Ooh, and I *have* to read what else Chase wrote. 'Best kiss of my life!'"

Ashley put a hand to her heart. How could she possibly resist him?

The crowd was going nuts and chanting, "Kiss, kiss, kiss!"

The other couples had simply leaned back and given a peck. Chase stood, walked around, knelt straight and strong in front of her and framed her face with his hands. Ashley sucked in a breath as the audience went still and anticipation filled the large room. She bent down as Chase arched up and their lips met. A flood of warmth and happiness swirled through her. Everyone in the world disappeared but the two of them.

Someone tapped her arm and then tugged them apart. Ashley caught a breath, lost in Chase's blue eyes.

"Wowzers!" Raoul hollered. "I can see why a kiss like that would be the best kiss of your life. These two have more chemistry than all of Hollywood." He fanned himself. "Whew. I guess somehow we've got to move on."

The crowd cheered.

Chase brushed his thumb along her cheek and murmured, "Let's get every answer correct."

Ashley's stomach filled with happy butterflies. "I plan on it."

Chase's grin made him even more handsome as he stood and strode around to his seat. Ashley hated letting him go.

"Second question," Raoul called out. "Where did you meet?"

Ashley was still swirling from that kiss, but easily wrote the answer out even though her hand was unsteady. Raoul went through the other couples. The newlywed couple got in a semi-fight, disagreeing about where they'd met, but the other couples got it right. It was finally hers and Chase's turn. Would she get another heart-stopping kiss?

Raoul took her paper. "'Chase's dermatologist office. I had a nasty rash the first time he met me.'" Raoul howled at that. "Ooh, and he got to examine you? I love it!"

He took Chase's paper. "'My office. Ashley had a rash, but I'd never seen a more beautiful woman.' Ahh. I love these two. Kiss, kiss, kiss." He started the chant and the crowd happily joined in.

Ashley wondered if she should lean back or go to him, but Chase stood, walked around, and this time he leaned forward and rested his hands on each side of her shoulders, bracing himself on the chair. Her breath escaped in fast pants as his handsome face grew near and then he was kissing her. She was transported to light and happiness. At this moment, she couldn't imagine anything or anyone could hurt her, least of all this incredible man.

Raoul yanked Chase back, laughing. "You two are giving us quite the show!"

Ashley blushed and admitted, "Sorry. I lose my mind when he kisses me."

Chase's eyes widened, but then he gave her a tender smile that was almost as good as his kisses.

The twenty-year married wife smacked her husband. "You hardly kiss me anymore!"

Everyone laughed and Chase returned to his seat. Ashley was determined to get the next question right. She needed more of his kisses. A lot more.

"What does your spouse, or boyfriend, do to annoy you? You have to write it both ways this time," he explained. "What you think you do to annoy and what he or she does to annoy you. Does that make sense?"

Everyone nodded and started writing. Ashley couldn't think how to respond. Should she be honest? The answers started rolling in and were very humorous. From bathroom issues to snoring to flirting with sisters-in-law. Raoul had a lot of fun with that one as the husband protested vehemently. They were finally to her and she was afraid she wasn't going to get a kiss and she would reveal far too much about herself and her desires.

Raoul took her paper and lifted an eyebrow as he scanned it. He cleared his throat. "'I'm scared of commitment.' So that's what Ashley wrote that Chase might find annoying. Hmm. Those kisses don't look scared." Ashley could feel Chase tense up behind her. "And Ashley said, 'The only thing Chase has ever done to annoy me is not kiss me enough.' Oh-ho!" Raoul and the crowd all roared. "Yeah, baby! I hope he gets this one right so we can see more of that kissing."

Chase reached back and wrapped his hand around hers, giving it a gentle squeeze and saying, "I can definitely remedy that."

Ashley flushed with pleasure and excitement. What was happening? Who knew being on some crazy fake game show would flip everything on its head for them? Was she really brave enough to walk through the door Chase was flinging wide open for her?

Raoul read aloud, "Chase says, 'I think I annoy Ashley because I push too hard.' Hmm. Doesn't sound like she minds that, my friend."

Ashley felt awful. Of course Chase had noticed her reluctance. Could she explain to him without seeming like the biggest loser on the planet? Was she ready to open herself up like that?

"And he says—oooh, you're all going to love this. 'There is absolutely nothing Ashley does that annoys me. In my mind, she's perfect.' Ah, happy sigh, friends." The audience complied with an exaggerated sigh.

The older wife smacked her husband, who'd said that she snored like a bear with a head cold.

Ashley sighed herself. Was Chase only being kind? She was certain she'd annoyed him when she'd run away.

"So no kiss for our hot and heavy dating couple." Raoul continued on.

Ashley was deflated. She wanted Chase's kiss, badly. She vowed to do better on the next question.

"Where is the most unique place you've ever made ... whoopee?" Raoul cleared his throat and had the grace to look embarrassed, though Ashley knew he'd chosen the questions. "Um, this is supposed to be a family show, so keep it clean, folks."

Ashley froze. Why would Raoul put that question in there? Yikes. What would the Chadwicks think if they were here? They were a Christian family. Ashley hoped they wouldn't think she was endorsing some naughty question. She wrote quickly and clung to her paper. Her face and neck burned. The couples luckily did keep it clean and nobody put any graphic answers, but some of the spots were unique.

When Raoul got to her, he read the answer. "'Nowhere.' Oh. That's ... boring."

Ashley gave him a stern look and he smiled. He took Chase's paper and read aloud, "'Nowhere. We're waiting for marriage.' Wow. These two are a match made in heaven, aren't they? Let's give it up for them and see how good the kiss is on this one!"

The crowd cheered loudly. Ashley felt relieved that they'd gotten through the question. She also felt excitement to kiss him again, and an odd fear that he'd said they were waiting for marriage. She hardly knew him. Marriage? The word that defined her career had also been her secret terror since she'd left so many men standing at the altar—or, slightly better, ditched them before the wedding day. It was impossible to describe how humiliating and painful that had been, even though she'd initiated the breakup. Thinking she'd found the love of her life each time and then finding out they were a flirt, a cheater, and in three of the cases, lazy and with no future plans besides her providing for them.

Chase stood and walked around. This time, he took both of her hands in his, tugged her to her feet, and pulled her in tight. He gave her a smoldering look that should've been on the movie screen and then bowed his head and kissed her. This kiss was tender and sweet, reflecting the question they'd just dodged. Chase wasn't looking for some passionate hookup. He was willing to wait for her, for marriage. Ashley was still be terrified of the m-word and commitment, but Chase was willing to take things slow. She wrapped her arms tightly around his neck and took the kiss to the next level.

The crowd hooted and Raoul tugged on her arm, yanking her back to reality. Chase gently helped her back into her seat, winked secretively at her, and walked around to his seat.

Raoul laughed. "These two are giving us a better show than we ever planned on. Okay, next question. Describe what you thought of your spouse, or dating partner, in one word. This one has to go both ways again. What you thought and what you thought they thought. Wow, that's a tongue twister."

Ashley didn't have a clue what to write. She finally scribbled a couple of words down and hoped she didn't look stupid. She doubted they'd match, which made her irrationally sad.

Raoul got through everybody's answers, stopping to tease the funny ones. He lifted Ashley's paper from her hands. "Ashley says Chase thought she was 'crazy' when she first met him and she thought he was 'competent.' Well, that's the most boring description you could give of our fine-looking doc." He shook his head in disgust and grabbed Chase's paper. "Chase says Ashley thought he was 'overbearing.'"

Everybody laughed.

"And he thought she was 'tantalizing'"

Everyone roared at that.

"Whoo-ee!" Raoul yelled to be heard over the noise.

As they settled and Raoul expressed his disappointment about no kiss, Ashley leaned back and whispered, "How could you think that? I was covered in a rash and a mess."

Chase's cheek rubbed against hers and he said, "I think that word every time I see you." His voice turned husky. "Every time."

Ashley thought she'd explode. She was falling so hard and fast for this guy. Was that smart? When would reality hit?

"Okay, folks, last question." Raoul mercifully interrupted her stewing. "What would be your spouse's ideal vacation?"

Ashley had no idea. She knew from their one dinner conversation that he was very active. Hmm. When Raoul got to her, he arched an eyebrow and said, "Heli-skiing in Canada for Chase. Snorkeling in the Caribbean for Ashley. Hmm." He took Chase's paper and read, "Zip-lining through the jungles of Costa Rica for Chase. Snorkeling or beach time on an island for Ashley." He laughed. "It appears our handsome boyfriend knows his girl, but it's not being reciprocated."

Ashley sat there, stunned, as the show wrapped up. The couple married fifty years won free spa treatments and dinner at the steakhouse. She could feel Chase behind her. She wanted to spin around and kiss him, but ... How did he know she wanted to go to an island and snorkel?

It suddenly hit her. Chase wasn't the problem, and maybe her other fiancés hadn't been completely to blame either. She could not go down this route again. The image she invented of Chase waiting at the end of a wedding aisle in his tux while she ran the other direction made her want to cry. She couldn't do that to him.

Tears stung at her eyes and she didn't like herself much right now. She didn't want to talk everything out with Chase. She didn't want him to know she'd been engaged seven times and ran every time. She didn't want to hurt him when he seemed so great. It was highly possible he wasn't a flirt or a cheater. Maybe he could be the one to overcome her horror of committing for life, but this was all moving too fast. Falling in love at Christmas was far too familiar.

She needed to get away. Now.

Standing slowly, she turned.

Chase was smiling at her. "I think we did pretty great," he said. "I especially loved the kissing. Should we go back to my suite and work on that some more?"

Ashley gave a nervous laugh. She'd love nothing more than to kiss him until Christmas morning, but it wasn't going to happen. "I've got to go check on things for the dance party. Thanks for doing the show with me."

His eyes registered confusion and frustration, but he only nodded. "It was amazing."

He stared at her as if daring her to disagree.

She couldn't. Kissing him and hearing his answers had been amazing.

"I'll see you soon?" He stared at her as if asking for a commitment she couldn't give.

"Um, I'll be busy tonight and then tomorrow is going to be crazy with the weddings. If this stupid storm clears. Sorry." She turned to go, but Chase put his hand on her arm.

"Ashley." His voice was low, beseeching. "I meant those answers and those kisses. Did you?"

She swallowed hard and gazed into his too-blue eyes. "Chase ... it's not you, it's me. I'm a mess and I'm sorry." She pulled away, turned, and all but ran from him. Her answer had been lame and he probably hated her for being so hot and cold with him. She couldn't blame him. Not at all. At least breaking away from him now would hurt less than getting engaged at Christmas for the eighth time and hurting him worse when she flaked before the spring wedding.

CHAPTER SEVEN

Ashley got through the dance party and hurried to her room. Chase had disappeared. Not that she blamed him. She'd kissed him multiple times as if she meant it, then when he tried to see where they stood, she gave him the lame, "It's not you, it's me." Ugh! She wished it could be different, but she had to somehow protect his heart—and hers, if he really was a flirt and a player.

She was up several times during the night, watching half of the third Crusaders movie during one of her nighttime awakenings. Sadly, Bennett Pike reminded her of Chase. She had weird dreams about Chase fighting aliens for her when she finally did fall asleep.

She slept late and felt disoriented and awful as sun streamed through her window and hit her face.

Sun?

She sprang out of bed. Staring out the huge windows, she

looked at a world of white. It was pristine and beautiful and she wanted to get out in it.

She called Iris, Meredith, and Hope, reveling in the good news that the weddings would happen this afternoon and evening. She checked on everything from the flowers being shipped in from Missoula—the floral shop said their skies were clear and as soon as the plows did their job, they'd be on their way—to the cakes being made by a local friend of the Chadwicks, to the food being prepared by the steak house downstairs, to the setup crew from the resort who were all on standby for whatever she needed.

Glancing at the clock, she realized it was only nine a.m. The first wedding didn't start until five. She worried her lip. Should she insist the family come early and practice? The brides hadn't asked for that, but Ashley wanted everything to go off without a hitch.

She needed to get outside. She needed to go for a run. It would clear her head, settle her, and she could think through every last detail as she pounded through the miles.

Dressing in warm running gear, she put on her running shoes, wishing she'd thought to bring her spikes. It might be slick out there, but who cared? She'd be outside.

Hurrying out her door and down the hallway, she wondered which of these suites was Chase's and what he was doing. Did he hate her? Probably. Could she blame him? Nope.

A door swung open and the perfect, incredible man she'd been hoping to avoid strode out.

Chase stopped, obviously surprised to see her. His gaze swept over her and he said almost worshipfully, "Ashley ... See why I said you were tantalizing?"

Ashley's breath stuttered in her chest. "Oh, Chase."

He quickly changed the subject. "Are you running outside?"

She nodded.

"Do you want to run together?"

Did she ever, but she didn't think she could do that to him. Not that he was proposing, but she always fell in love at Christmas. If she could just get through this holiday and get back home, maybe she could observe him in different situations and make certain he wasn't a flirt. She could pursue him and see if she had finally found the one she wouldn't run away from.

She had to somehow stay strong and distanced from him, no matter how appealing he was. She shook her head, hating how his eyes dimmed. "I'm going crazy trying to make sure every last detail is perfect for the weddings. I need to run alone and think it all through."

"Oh," was all he said. He lifted a hand. "Good luck."

Ashley wished he'd beg her to run with him, to talk to him, to kiss him, but she was the one who kept rejecting him. She gave him a tight smile and hurried to the stairs, dashing down them. Within half a minute, she was through the foyer with only a wave at a front desk girl she didn't recognize and then into the sunshine. It looked like Daisy was able to get home to her family for Christmas. That was great.

The outside air was brisk, chilly on her cheeks, and so invigorating. She felt like she was escaping prison. If only she wasn't running from what might be the perfect man for her.

———

Chase gave a grunt of frustration, at himself and Ashley, and quietly followed her down the stairs. He'd spent a restless night worried about everything from Ashley to the Chadwicks to where in the world his mom was. He'd woken up at five a.m. as usual, lifted weights, and swam, hoping the entire time for Ashley to appear. After breakfast, he'd been stir-crazy and dying to get outside, so he'd dressed in workout clothes. It was sheer luck that he'd seen Ashley. Or was it luck?

When he exited the resort, he relished the bright sun on his face and the chill in the air. It felt good to be outside. He looked right and left and saw Ashley running toward the west, away from town and toward the cabins circling the lake. He gave her a few beats and then followed at a steady pace. Every so often, he caught her bright red running shirt through a break in the trees. She was running on the road. It had been plowed, but it wasn't clear. It was hard-packed snow that wasn't bad to run on.

If only he knew why he was such a wimp. Why did he continually chase a woman who didn't want to be chased? Plenty of women wanted him to chase them, but did he care? No. He wanted the one he couldn't have. That had to say something about him. Was it because he had no father? Was it because his mom wasn't returning his calls and so maybe he had no mother anymore? That worry was growing in his mind, but he said a prayer and tried to tamp down the rising concern. No reason to borrow trouble, as his mom would say. There seemed to be a lot of trouble coming at him no matter what he did.

They'd probably run over three miles and Ashley wasn't slowing down. Chase was impressed, and wished he dared approach her, kiss her, beg to know why she kept dodging and ditching him. He had this unreasonable hope that if he could talk Ashley into dating him, he could deal with introducing himself to the Chadwicks as their most likely unwanted son and brother and even deal with whatever was making his mom absentee.

A dark shape raced through the trees to his left. Chase was pulled from his own worries and instantly concerned for Ashley. It had to be an animal, but what was it? Was it headed for Ashley?

He could see her red shirt bobbing away from him and then that dark shape racing after her. He upped his speed right as he heard a low growl that made his spine prickle.

"Ashley!" he hollered in warning as he sprinted after her and whatever was about to attack her. He cleared the stand of trees and was racing along the road.

"Chase?" She stopped and turned to face him just as the black animal plowed into her, knocking her onto the snowy bank on the side of the road.

"Ashley!" he called, dodging toward her.

He heard a loud bark and Ashley's cry for help. He was almost upon her and he could see the wagging tail of a huge black dog.

"Go! Stop!" Ashley cried out. "Help!"

Chase grabbed the dog's collar and ripped the animal off of Ashley. The dog was huge, probably almost a hundred and fifty pounds, but his adrenaline was rushing through him. The dog whimpered in surprise and nestled against his leg, panting for attention. He was a Great Dane, known for their mild temperaments. He didn't seem to be a threat. Chase released the dog's collar and bent down for Ashley, lifting her out of the snow and into his arms.

"Are you okay?" he asked.

"I think so." She seemed to evaluate and then said, "He didn't bite me or anything, but he was heavy. It scared me and I flipped out." She glanced up at him. "You rescued me."

Then she flung her arms around his neck and kissed him.

Chase didn't feel the cold or his worries any longer. The dog pressed into his leg and whined for attention, but no way was Chase giving up this kiss for any kind of distraction. He cradled Ashley close and deepened the kiss. She responded, oh how she responded, and he felt like he would never come down from the happy spot he was soaring to. Everything would work out. He knew it in that moment.

"Hey!" an angry voice hollered from the trees.

Chase released Ashley from the kiss and hurriedly ushered her behind him, turning to face the new threat.

"Get away from my dog," the man yelled.

Interestingly, the Great Dane cowered against Chase rather than trotting to its owner.

A man stormed through the trees. He was wearing joggers and a fitted long-sleeved shirt that displayed all his glamour muscles. His blond hair was slicked back from a model-looking face. Chase's army buddies would call him a pretty boy.

"What are you doing with my dog?" he demanded.

"He chased Ashley and knocked her over. We didn't hurt the dog," Chase said in a calm voice, trying to diffuse the situation. He didn't mind fighting anybody and he hated to pre-judge, but his Army friends would also say this guy had a very punchable face—he had girl-fake eyebrows and looked far too cocky with his skin-tight shirt. Chase didn't want to fight right now though. He wanted to get Ashley alone and see if they could keep kissing and make sure she didn't push him away again.

"You stupid dog." The man let out a few choice swear words, then demanded, "Get on over here, you mutt." The man's coarse manner didn't match his high-dollar clothes and primped face and body.

Ashley tried to edge around Chase, but he held her back. She poked her head around and said, "That's no way to talk to that dog."

The man growled at her and started their direction, but he must've gotten a glimpse of Ashley because his face changed instantly. He puffed out his well-built chest and said, "Oh ... hey, pretty girl. I can talk sweet to the dog, and you too, if that's what you'd like."

"Back off," Chase warned with a command he'd perfected in the military.

The guy only looked slightly concerned and took an idiotic step forward.

Chase tensed for battle.

"Pepper," a female voice called and then a woman material-ized from behind a tree. Chase's eyes widened as he realized who it was. The dog quickly left Chase's side with a friendly "ruff" of goodbye and bounded over to none other than Kris Bellissima. She was wearing a thick robe, boots, and a beanie over her dark curls, but her robe was undone enough to see her bra and bosom.

"Kris?" he questioned. She was the last person he expected to see, but he would love to get some answers from her. If she really had any information about his family.

He must've relaxed his grip on her arm because Ashley moved slightly away from him.

Kris batted her eyelashes at him as she stroked the dog's back. "Hey, Chase. I'm so glad you found me. I'm about fed up with this jerk." She tilted her head toward the man. "I preferred being alone with you at my suite at the resort." She licked her lips. "You remember, don't you? You stud."

"You are such a slut," the man roared. "Any good-looking guy comes along and you flirt with him. I come all this way and bring your mutt to you because 'you can't live without Pepper for

Christmas,'" he said in a false soprano, "and this is the thanks I get."

"You just hit on the blonde, you idiot," she yelled right back. The dog whimpered and she petted him more furiously. "It's okay, Pepper. I won't let him hurt you."

Chase blew out a breath. Did he need to intervene or get Ashley out of here?

Ashley edged away from him and he glanced down. "I've got to get back to the resort. Plan the weddings," she said quietly.

He wanted to run with her, but ice rubbed at his spine when Kris said, "Please don't leave, Chase. Aaron likes to hit me."

Aaron responded with a string of profanity that made Chase's stomach curdle. Chase nodded to Ashley. "Get back to the resort. I'll help Kris."

"Okay." She didn't even attempt a smile as she turned and ran back up the road, probably relieved to get away from all of this.

"You are hot," Aaron hollered after Ashley. "Hate to see you leaving, but love watching you go."

That was it. Chase flew at the idiot, starting with a quick jab to his nose. He felt it snap and then blood was flowing down the guy's face. Aaron screamed in pain and cursed as vile as any man Chase had served in the military with.

Kris hurried to them, grabbed Aaron's arm, and stared at Chase. "What are you *doing*?"

"You said he hits you." Chase stated the obvious. "And he has no right to be checking out Ashley or saying stupid lines to her."

"I'll sue you," Aaron squealed.

Kris let out a long-suffering sigh. "I only said he hits me so *you'd* give me some attention. Who's the blonde? Ashley? She doesn't deserve you. She looks like a pastor's daughter, all innocent and lame."

"Don't talk about Ashley," Chase said in a low voice.

"Does anyone care about me here?" Aaron asked, his speech slightly slurred with the blood he was probably swallowing. "He broke my nose."

"You are such a wimp," Kris tossed at him. "Come on, let's go doctor you up." She blinked up at Chase. "Can I see you later?"

"No." He rolled his eyes at this insane situation. He'd lost an opportunity with Ashley and for what? Kris flirting with him again. He'd thought she was impressive and classy when he looked her up on social media after she'd contacted him last week, but she was disgusting and vile in real life. He doubted any information she had about his family would even be true.

Kris's overly full lips almost went thin. "You can't really not want me. Every man in America wants me."

"Not me," he insisted. He inclined his head to Aaron. "Are you in danger with him?"

"No," Kris admitted, tossing her boyfriend a contemptuous look.

Aaron threw his hands in the air. "I ain't never hit her, though she probably deserves it, always stepping out on me and making me crazy jealous. First with that hotshot Quill Chadwick and then with that loser Todd Plowman."

"No interest in a Christmas kiss?" Kris asked, plumping up her lips again and completely ignoring her idiotic boyfriend.

"No." Chase turned away in disgust.

"Did you talk to your brother Quill then?" Kris asked to his back.

That got him to spin back around. "No," he admitted. "Are you certain he's my brother?"

She nodded.

"How do you know?" He really didn't trust her or her info.

"Come on over here and I'll share *all* my info." She winked lewdly at him.

Chase backed up. He'd much rather try to find Quill or one of the other siblings himself than get close to her again. Now that the storm was over, they'd return to the resort. He wouldn't interrupt the weddings, but maybe tomorrow he'd have some answers. If only his mom would answer her phone.

"Come on, babe," Aaron whined. "It hurts. I need ice, and a beer, and some painkillers, and some of your lips on me."

Chase turned and started to run on the road back toward the resort. Those two were ridiculous. He wanted to find Ashley again, but Kris's words were ringing in his head. How could she know Quill was his brother? He needed answers, but he didn't think Kris had them. Was she so interested in him because she couldn't have Quill? She was a crazy diva, that was for sure.

He was almost to the resort when his phone rang. He pulled it out of his pocket and sighed. Next to Ashley, this was the woman he wanted to talk to most. He let out a breath of relief and a quick prayer of thanks.

"Mom! Are you okay? Why haven't you answered the phone?" He felt like the over-worried parent. His mom was okay. He was so relieved, he had to stop moving for a minute.

"Handsome Rob! I'm fine, love. How's my baby boy?"

He chuckled. "Not great. I've been worried about you."

"I'm so sorry I haven't called. Ned and I ... well, we got married."

"Mom!" That explained why she had been out of pocket. Nobody deserved to be happy as much as his mom. He couldn't begrudge her not returning his call. Though it would've been nice to know she wasn't hanging off a mountain somewhere. Now if only he wasn't such a mess himself. "That is fabulous news. Tell Ned congrats. You two are amazing together."

"Aw, thanks, love. That means a lot. Sorry we didn't get you down here for it. Once Ned got me to latch on to the idea, I found I didn't want to wait one more second. I really love him. I never thought I'd love anyone again after …"

Chase waited. Was this it? Was she going to tell him who his dad was?

"Anyway. We're so happy. We went and stayed in this beautiful house up in the cloud forest and left all of our devices back at our house on the beach so we could just focus on each other. What's going on with you? Why aren't you great? I'm missing you, my boy! Tell me all, love."

"Mom." Chase walked along the road to the resort and figured if she was happy and in love, now might be the time to ask. "I need to know who my father is."

Stony silence met his request. Chase waited. When his mom spoke, her voice was so quiet he barely picked it up. "Why would you ruin my marriage and Christmas with a request like that?"

Chase heaved out a loud breath. "Mom, you know I adore you and only want you happy, but some information has come to light and I need to know if the Chadwick family who own Mystical Lake Resort are my half-siblings."

The silence stretched. He approached the resort while he waited. Even though it was bitter cold outside, he paced the parking lot.

Finally, she said in a low voice, "Yes, they are."

The air whooshed out of him and Chase had to stop walking and catch his breath. It was true. He had an entire family that he'd never known. The faces he'd found online went through his mind: Aster, Cedar, Quill, Ren, and Iris. Was his dad really gone?

Where? How did he approach them all without flipping them out completely?

"Are you all right?" his mom asked.

"It's just a lot to take in," he said. "Why didn't you ever tell me?"

A long pause. "I was humiliated that I'd slept with a married man who had a family. I had no clue he was married. He lived in Mystical Lake, so he only came to be with me on the weekends during my short summer break. I told him I was pregnant and he begged me to stay away from him and not hurt his beloved wife and ruin his family. He wanted me to give you up for adoption, but I couldn't let you go. I never wanted you to know that your dad ... didn't want to be a part of your life. I never wanted you to feel like less." Her voice dropped, trembling as she said, "I hoped I was enough for you and you'd never feel the loss of not having a father."

"Oh, Mom." Chase pushed a hand through his hair and went back to pacing the parking lot. "Of course you're enough. You were amazing and I had a great childhood."

But of course he'd wanted a dad like his friends had. What little boy wouldn't?

"Thank you, love." There was another long pause, then she asked, "Are you going to talk to him ... Peter? I don't know how he'll act with you, sweetie."

"Oh." He continued walking. His dad might not want him, but he didn't think Peter was in the valley anyway. When he and Ashley had talked about the Chadwicks, she'd talked about everyone, even Uncle Jay, but never Peter.

He wanted to focus on his siblings. A dad had always seemed like a fictional character to him anyway, but he had lots of friends and Army buddies who felt like brothers. Brothers he could wrap his mind around. A sister sounded even more incredible. Would they reject him?

"I don't think he's around."

"Oh, that's ... I don't know what to say or think, sweetheart."

"I can understand that." Clinging to the phone with chilled fingers, he asked, "Do you care if I approach some of my half-siblings? If it feels right?"

"It's okay with me. I hope they're nice to you, love. I'm so sorry that my poor choices are putting you in an awkward spot."

That was odd to think about. Her "poor choices" had also created him, so he felt a little conflicted about her choice of words. But he knew she didn't mean it like that. She'd chosen him and adored him, always.

"If they aren't welcoming," she continued, "just know that they are idiots. You're the best man I know and I couldn't be more proud of you."

"Thanks, Mom." He appreciated her words, but he was suddenly apprehensive about introducing himself to the Chadwicks. What if they didn't want him around? What if this news messed up their wedding days and Christmas? Suddenly he wanted to hide, wait for the right time. Who knew when that would be?

For the first time, he wasn't stewing about Ashley.

He didn't like the change.

CHAPTER EIGHT

Ashley didn't see or hear from Chase the rest of the day. She wasn't surprised. That woman with her chest hanging out had been Kris Bellissima. She'd obviously been interested in Chase, and that awful man was hurting the famous woman, "America's sweetheart" as Kris was often called. Chase needed to protect Kris, but it made Ashley sick. She was pretty certain Kris was the same woman who had pulled him into her hotel suite early in the week wanting him to "get his handsome body" in the room with her.

She was a stirred-up mess where Chase was concerned anyway, so she should be grateful for the break. She wasn't.

Instead of worrying about it, she focused all her energy on the weddings. Wedding practice took place in the afternoon, followed by the tender and joyful weddings of Iris and Devon, followed by Cruz and Meredith, and finishing with Cedar and Hope.

The weddings were beautiful and perfect. The dinner and

dancing and cake-cutting and bouquet-throwing were everything any bride could hope for. All of it was textbook wonderful and as she fell into bed late on the night of December twenty-third, Ashley knew she should be ecstatic.

But all she could think about was Chase.

Where had he disappeared to? Was he with Kris? Ashley wished she could chase him down, but she was too confused and stirred up to even know how to make a relationship work. If Chase was even still interested.

What should she do with herself now? She was in charge of the Christmas Eve party tomorrow for the entire Chadwick family, the people from town, and everyone at the resort. She had this suite until the New Year, but it seemed silly to stay in Mystical Lake throughout the holidays by herself. The Chadwicks would of course welcome her as part of their own family, but her family was in Missoula. They would be thrilled if she drove home late Christmas Eve.

Christmas Eve dawned sunny and bright. She woke with new resolve. Maybe Chase was dating Kris Bellissima, but probably not. That awful blond man who looked so handsome but had been such a jerk had been with Kris. Chase had probably stayed there to protect Kris, not because he was in love with her. As Ashley thought through every interaction she'd had with Chase, and the times she'd seen other women hit on him, it seemed he truly was only interested in Ashley.

Maybe Ashley could never be in a functional relationship because of her weird commitment issues. It wasn't fair to Chase, but she wanted to at least talk to him about it. If she told him about her prior engagements and he didn't want to risk being in a relationship that would take a lot of work from both of them, she would understand. At this moment, though, talking it through was a positive step. She got excited thinking about it. Could Chase be the one to break through her commitment issues?

It was five a.m. and she wondered if Chase might be in the gym or the swimming pool as he'd been on other mornings. Just to cover all her bases, she changed into a sporty swimsuit with a tank top and shorts over the top. She slid into socks and tied her shoes, then ran down the hall and the stairs and into the gym. It was empty.

She hurried out the door and looked into the windows of each of the indoor pools. Empty.

Shoulders rounded, she trudged back to the gym. She warmed up halfheartedly on the elliptical machine. It was Christmas Eve and she was alone. She'd be busy throughout the day with the Chadwicks' party, but she'd still be alone. Chase had rescued her yesterday and the kisses they'd shared had her lips hoping for more, but she was such a head case. She had no idea if she could ever make a relationship work. Maybe he was avoiding her now. It made complete sense. Did she dare go knock on his suite door? At five a.m. on Christmas Eve? Most sane people were sleeping in.

The door opened and the subject of her thoughts walked in. He looked like hot man on a stick in a t-shirt and shorts, his dark hair tousled and his blue eyes focused in on her. He didn't need tight clothes or fake eyebrows like that other guy to show off his muscles and be handsome. His eyes looked tortured yet hopeful.

"Hey," she called out happily. "Merry Christmas!"

"Hey." He raised a hand, looking confused by her warm greeting. "Are you okay? After ... yesterday?"

"Yes." She nodded and got off the elliptical machine, walking to him. He didn't back away or anything, but something was definitely off. "Are you okay?"

He shrugged. "I had some weird stuff happen yesterday. I'm just trying to work it all out in my mind."

"Oh." She shifted from foot to foot, suddenly awkward and uncomfortable. So maybe he did want Kris and was confused by his feelings? "Is there, um, anything I can do to help?"

He studied her. "You would want to help me?"

"Well, yeah. You've been very kind to me." She gave him what she hoped was an appealing smile. "Rescuing me from that dog and weird guy yesterday. Being my boyfriend on the newlywed game." Kissing her over and over again.

He licked his lips and admitted, "You've given me a lot of mixed signals."

She backed up a step, stunned by his honesty. "You're right. I have."

"Now you want to talk about it?"

She glanced around at the empty gym. Not right now. "Here?" Her throat felt thick and uncomfortable at the thought of spilling it all.

She could see the frustration in his blue eyes, felt it radiating off of him. "I'm afraid if I don't pin you down right here, you'll run off again and I won't be able to find you."

"You want me to tell you all my secrets?"

"Yes, I do." He folded his arms across his chest. His biceps bulged. It should've been intimidating, but she knew he was a nice guy. He'd hit that jerk yesterday, but the guy had it coming.

Was she ready to tell him about her lame almost-marriages and the reasons she had been so cold and hot with him? She had to be honest and admit that most of her failures were her own fault. What would he think of her after she revealed all?

"Are you going to tell me your secrets too?" she asked to give herself time. There was something secretive about the "hard" conversation he had to have with someone the other day, his relationship with Kris Bellissima—whatever it was—and his odd change in personality today.

A muscle twitched in his jaw. His voice lowered. "Ashley, I am very, very interested in you, but can you see that you've been very hot and cold with me? You've sent a lot of mixed signals."

"Yes," she said miserably.

He studied her, then said, "What does your day look like?"

"Busy," she admitted. "I've got to organize a bunch of party favors and games and run the Christmas Eve party this afternoon and evening."

"When will you be able to talk?"

"Can we have dinner together?"

"I would like that." He tucked a strand of hair behind her ear and she trembled from even that simple touch. "I'll tell you my secrets and you'll tell me yours."

"It's a plan," she said before she could wimp out and run. "Six?"

"Yes."

She tried to nod bravely, but inside she was terrified. She didn't like the idea of sharing her secrets. She hadn't shared them with anyone. Her fiancés had eventually known how many times she'd been engaged. Most of them had teased her about it, certain they'd be the one to break the "curse." Brandon had made fun of her when he found out. Called her his "Runaway Bride" and cockily told everyone he was the only man who could pin her down. She would've felt bad about dumping him at the altar, if he hadn't cheated on her with multiple women.

Her family knew what had happened and supported her time

and again. Sadly, she had no close friends. Maybe that was part
of her lack of commitment too. She was so busy and invested
with work that she always had a new bride, or dozens depending
on the season, to be her close friends as they worked together
throughout the wedding planning. She still kept in contact with
many of her brides, but she was the epitome of cheering, listening, solving their problems without telling anyone much about
herself.

She hated these reflections. How much should she share with
Chase? Would her past, her secrets, the way she interacted with
others make her seem pathetic to Chase? Would he realize she
wasn't capable of a lasting relationship?

Either way, baring her soul sounded very, very scary.

———

Chase spent a long day trying to stay busy just like yesterday.
Luckily, today he could get outside. He borrowed some snow-
shoes from the front desk and went on a three-hour adventure
through the mountains. He found some of his basketball-playing
friends and ate a late lunch with them, then bundled up and
joined the snow-sledding activity the resort was hosting. They
had snowmobiles pulling everyone to the top of a hill near the
resort and then tubes to fly down. It was fun acting like a kid
again. He saw Ashley running around, but she only waved.
Between worrying how their conversation would go tonight and
wondering if he should just walk up to one of the Chadwicks and
tell them who he was, he was a mess.

He saw some of the Chadwick family members, but not
Quill. He wasn't sure why, but he felt like Quill was the one he
needed to approach because of his connection to Kris. He could

still remember the scandal when Kris's hockey player boyfriend Todd Plowman had lied to her. She had claimed Quill was the one who threw hockey games for gambling purposes, but it was actually Todd. Kris and especially Quill had handled the situation with extreme maturity, so Chase assumed there was no bad blood between them. Now that he'd gotten to know Kris a little bit, Chase wondered what the true story was.

After sledding, he got some hot cocoa and donuts. The brunette from the gym yesterday morning was circling like a buzzard ready to dive on her prey, giving him sultry looks and blinking her long eyelashes.

He dodged behind groups of children and all but ran for the safety of the lodge. He had this irrational feeling that if he could just make it until dinner time, all this angst and worry would go away. Ashley would tell him her secrets and why she'd been so hot and cold. He'd reveal to her that he was falling for her and wanted to date her. When she agreed to date him, and after they kissed for a few hours, he could tell her he was related to the Chadwicks and together maybe they could talk to his half-siblings, figure out where his dad was. Even if the Chadwicks didn't want him, he would have Ashley with him. It was all unknown territory, but it would be much easier to approach the Chadwicks with Ashley by his side.

Everything sounded better with her by his side.

He had to have faith that it would all work out. As he got to his room, he hit his knees and prayed. He needed patience, insight, and understanding. Not just about how to approach the family he'd never known existed, but how to work things out with Ashley. He'd never been so invested in a woman before, but she obviously had hang-ups. At least she was willing to talk it through at dinner.

After a long prayer, he put on comfortable clothes and found a group playing pickleball who was willing to let him join. Not his usual buddies, but it was still fun.

Finally, he made it to five-thirty and hurried up to his suite to shower. They hadn't decided on a place for dinner, but the entire resort was one big party, so he'd probably find her on the main floor near the food somewhere. He dressed in a button-down white shirt, tie, and navy blue slacks. He sprayed on some of his favorite 18.21 Manmade cologne and said another quick prayer before heading out the door.

He was going to head for the elevator but took a chance and hurried to her suite door. Rapping his knuckles on the wood, he rubbed his palms against his pants to make sure they weren't sweaty. He was nervous, legitimately so. Between being in the Army and competing in a demanding specialty after medical school, he'd learned not to allow nerves to distract him. But he was a mess for Ashley and who could blame him? When she wasn't running away, she was amazing.

The door swung open and his nerves ramped up. Ashley stood there in a red dress that swirled perfectly around her curves. It was alluring without being too tight and with her long, blonde curls and blue eyes lighting up as she saw him, he was pretty certain he'd just found heaven.

"Hey," he said softly.

"Hey." She tucked her hair behind her ear. He worked on skin conditions all day and he'd participated in numerous research studies on skin, but the smoothness of her skin and her soft lips were more appealing and perfect than anything he'd ever seen.

He wanted to say something brilliant, or at least beg her to love him until the day he died.

"Dinner?" was all he could think to spit out.

She smiled and he extended his hand. She took it and he felt like Bennett Pike's overconfident, tough character Sword Ace escorting her down the hallway and to the elevator. Nervous excitement arced between them. He couldn't be the only one who felt it. This was their night, their time. They were going to share all their secrets and somehow, some way, he would get a commitment out of her.

Neither of them said anything on the elevator ride down. He snuck glances at her and she met his gaze with this beautiful, almost shy look and then quickly looked away. His nerves were amped up in the best possible way. He still wanted to connect with the Chadwicks soon, but Ashley was his priority. All that mattered right now was connecting with her.

He escorted her from the elevator and toward the restaurants. "There they are," Raoul called out happily as they approached his maître d' stand. "Ah, you two make my heart happy."

"Do you ever take time off?" Ashley asked.

He smiled. "I'm married to my job and I love it. Soon I will be the assistant manager." He winked and then tsked. "Unfortunately, your romantic table in the back corner of my restaurant is occupied." He gestured to tables set up throughout the main area with the huge party going on. "Is one of these all right?"

Chase didn't love how exposed those tables felt but some were out of the way, up against the huge windows overlooking the lake. "Can we get the quietest one?"

The party was in full swing. Couples were dancing and food and treats were everywhere.

"Of course. Follow me." Raoul led them to a table for two nestled against the windows. It wasn't as private as Chase would've liked, but it was all right. "I feel wonderful about you two," Raoul said, giving Chase a slap on the back as he set menus down and left.

"Thanks, Raoul." Chase got Ashley's chair and then sat. Staring at her as she picked up the menu, he wondered where to start and how to make sure he didn't scare her away again.

She looked up and gave him an embarrassed smile. "Don't you want to look at the menu and see what you want?"

He studied her. "I already know what I want."

Her eyebrows arched. "What's that?"

"You."

She pulled in a quick breath and her pulse fluttered like mad in her neck. Chase suddenly didn't care about dinner. He'd starve. He only wanted to be alone with her, to share and listen to secrets, and then to kiss the night away, sealing the promise they would both make to be together. Was that possible?

"Chase." She released her menu and put a hand to her chest. Her voice trembled. "I'm afraid when you hear my secrets you won't want anything to do with me."

"There is no chance of that."

Two large shadows loomed over them. Chase looked up and recognized Cedar Chadwick. The other man was unfamiliar, but he looked debonair, like a James Bond type of dude. Maybe he was Iris's new husband. Chase had hidden behind a potted plant at the weddings, so he hadn't had a clear view. He hadn't wanted to mess up his siblings' wedding days by shocking and possibly hurting them with the news of their unknown brother. Would he ruin their Christmas instead?

"Hey, man," Cedar said. "Sorry to interrupt, but Grams saw you and Ashley walk in and she has completely lost her mind. Do you have a minute to help us find it?"

Chase looked over at Ashley. Her eyes were wide and

confused, but as she looked from Cedar to Chase and back a couple times, something seemed to click. She put her hand to her mouth and then asked quietly, "Why didn't you tell me?"

Cedar glanced down at her. "Is this guy an imposter?"

Ashley lifted her hands and shoulders. "I don't think so. I don't know. I never recognized the resemblance until just now."

"Can you please come talk to Grams before she completely flips out?" Cedar asked.

Chase was torn. He'd come here to find and talk to his family and now they'd sought him out. But if he turned his back, would Ashley run like she had every single time? He wanted to beg her to stay right here or come with him, but he didn't know what to say with these men watching. He stood and said to Ashley, "I'll be right back."

She stared at him as if she wasn't certain who he was anymore.

Chase felt full of frustration, but now wasn't the time. Cedar and the other guy stood on either side of him. They strode toward a knot of Chadwick family members.

A beautiful, pipsqueak of a lady with silver-gray hair stared up at him and demanded, "Who are you and where did you get those blue eyes? What are you doing hiding that handsome face behind a beard?"

It was time to face the music. Chase glanced back at Ashley. She hadn't left the table. Would she wait for him? He'd prefer she stood by his side, but there wasn't time to ask that of her.

He cleared his throat and looked around at all the interested faces. His gaze lit on a gorgeous blonde with blue eyes. Iris. His baby sister. The James Bond-looking guy had his arm around her, but those blue eyes were so familiar to him, as if they were his own. She looked so innocent and welcoming. He really,

really wanted to be part of her life. A little sister of his very own.

"My mother is a dermatologist in Missoula," he began. "Wren Hamilton. When she was in medical school, she came home for a short summer break and dated a man named Peter Chadwick. They became ... very close." Did he have to spell out that he was the result of that closeness?

Everyone sucked in a collective breath.

"How old are you?" the older lady demanded.

"Well, ma'am..."

"It's Grams to you."

He felt warmth erupt inside him. Even though she was obviously upset, she knew who he was and she was ready to claim him as her own.

"Grams." He smiled at her, hoping it didn't look like a grimace from how stirred up he was. He checked Ashley's position. She hadn't moved, sipping on her water. He looked back at the pretty blonde. His sister. "I'm thirty-one."

There was an eruption of muttering and questions. Chase focused on the man standing next to him. Aster, he was pretty sure. The oldest Chadwick brother. He looked tough, like a construction worker. Where was Quill? For some reason, he wanted Quill to be here.

"Right smack between Quill and Ren," Aster muttered, his fist clenching. "The scum-ball."

"Excuse me?" Maybe Chase wasn't as welcome with his siblings as he might have hoped.

"Not you. Our father." Aster met his gaze. "Your father too, right?"

Everyone was listening. Chase cleared his throat. "My mom never told me who my father was, no matter how many times I asked, but Kris Bellissima lured me here. She said she had information about my half-brother, Quill Chadwick."

That caused another stir. A petite beauty with dark skin and hair and unique green eyes gave him a look that said he had ticked her off. Oh man, he was stepping on landmines everywhere.

Grams was staring expectantly at him, so he continued. "My mother finally admitted the truth to me yesterday."

"Why would she keep you from us?" Iris asked with a cute little fist planted on her waist.

His sister wanted him in their lives? That made him feel warm inside. "Peter begged her to give me up for adoption and not ruin his family. She left to finish her last year of medical school. She told me she couldn't give me up. She had me two days after she graduated."

"You're my grandson?" Grams asked with a waver in her voice.

He nodded shortly, somewhat terrified of her response. He wasn't trying to ruin anyone's Christmas or come in as the stain on the family that they didn't want to talk about.

"You're my grandson," Grams repeated. Her blue eyes were bright as she marched up to him and opened her arms.

He bent down and wrapped his arms around her. Grams hugged him fiercely, as if making up for thirty-one years of lost hugs. Tears streamed down her weathered cheeks. His own eyes grew moist, his throat was thick with emotion. He already had grandparents. His mom's parents had been great to him. They had always helped his mom as much as they could without raising him or crippling his mom's passion about being self-reliant. But it wasn't possible for a body to have too much love and he knew—deep down, he knew—that Grams loved him.

When she released him, the other family members moved in for hugs, questions, and expressions of acceptance. It felt amazing. He had lots of friends, but expanding his family circle was incredible.

They almost went in order: Aster and his wife Chelsea, Cedar and his wife Hope, Iris and her new husband Devon. He also met Uncle Jay, his cousins Cruz and Cat and their spouses, as well as Ren's girlfriend Mavyn who was the saucy brunette with green eyes. She demanded information about Kris.

Apparently, Ren was off fighting a fire and Quill and his girlfriend, Cora, were at his hockey game. Grams said that Chase could meet Quill and Cora tomorrow if he'd come to her house for Christmas.

As the excitement and the questions slowed, he wanted them all to meet Ashley, but then he remembered they knew Ashley. She was their wedding and party planner. He turned to find her, bring her into this circle of welcome and acceptance, but she was gone. He almost cursed. He'd thought tonight would be his chance to finally connect with her. He was thrilled to be with his family, but missing out on Ashley sharing her secrets and him sharing his was a punch to the gut.

"Do you think your mom would want to come meet us?" Grams asked. "We wouldn't want to push her too hard, but she's our family too, right?"

"I think she would like to meet all of you, but ..." Chase looked around at all the interested faces. "I wouldn't want to upset Peter or taint the memory of your mom." He nodded to Aster, Cedar, and Iris.

Aster's brow furrowed. "Thanks, but it's not Mom's fault our dad cheated." Chase appreciated that they didn't seem worried about how people in the town would perceive them. "Dad's in

South America. I doubt he'll ever come back." His voice lowered. "So you knew Mom passed away twelve years ago?"

"Yes. I'm sorry about your mom."

They all nodded their acceptance of that statement.

"We're sorry you didn't have a dad growing up," Iris said. "Our dad left when I was sixteen and it sucked."

Chase smiled at her. "I always wanted a dad. For a while, I talked myself into believing my dad was Santa Claus." Everybody laughed. "But I was okay. My mom is a strong, impressive lady and she was always there for me."

Cedar nodded. "Our mom was a rock star too."

There was a pause as if they were all honoring their moms. There was a still a hole left from their dad disappearing, but at least they could weather it together.

Grams broke the silence. "This is a party! I want to dance with my new grandson and eat some chocolate cake."

Chase grinned and took his small grandmother in his arms for a waltz around the room. She grinned up at him. "You're every bit as handsome as my other boys, but maybe you could shave that face."

He laughed. "You don't like the beard, Grams?"

"No. But I like every part of you, so it's okay if you want to keep the beard."

Chase chuckled. He automatically loved her too. He'd never thought about shaving the beard, but maybe he'd do it for Grams. Everything about the reveal and his new family felt great. If only Ashley hadn't disappeared. He frowned as he looked around for her again.

"What are you messing up that handsome face for by frowning so big?" Grams asked.

"I was eating dinner with Ashley Casey, the wedding planner, when Cedar and Devon came for me."

"Oh ... Sorry, that was my fault. I couldn't wait one more second. You love our darling Ashley?"

"Well, love is a bit premature, but I'm definitely falling for her and want to date her."

"This is the best Christmas I've had in a long time. Let's talk turkey, my boy. I know exactly what you need to do to get her smooching on you."

Chase laughed again, but he listened intently to her advice.

It wasn't anything earth-shattering, but it just might work.

CHAPTER NINE

Ashley watched Chase reconnect with his family. She was happy for him. This wasn't the moment for the two of them to talk everything out. It was crazy that she hadn't known he'd come to Mystical Lake to connect with his half-siblings, cousins, and grandmother. During their dinner date, he'd asked questions about the Chadwicks, but they were an interesting family, so she hadn't thought much of it. Was it crazy to wonder if he'd been hanging around her to get an introduction to his family?

She slipped away and headed back to her room, changing out of her dress and reading through the latest issue of *Modern Bride* to distract herself.

A knock at her door brought her head up. She jumped out of the chair she'd been lounging in, straightening her t-shirt and wishing she wasn't wearing yoga pants. Hurrying to the door, she flung it open. Chase stood there with Raoul. Raoul was grinning, but Chase looked a little apprehensive. He held flowers in one hand and a bag of chocolate caramels in the other. Raoul had one hand on the handle of a room service cart.

"Hey, Ashley," Raoul said brightly, pushing the cart past her into the room and busying himself unloading covered platters onto her table.

"Hey." Chase didn't walk in, instead extending the flowers and the chocolates. His blue eyes were serious and questioning. "Could I eat dinner with you? Somehow I missed my dinner date."

She clutched the flowers in one hand and the box of chocolates in the other. Taking a second to smell the fragrant mixture of roses, daisies, and lilacs, she asked, "How'd you know chocolate caramels were my favorite?"

Chase's eyebrows lifted. "Lucky. They're my mom's favorite and they had them in the gift shop."

"Well." Raoul bustled past them in the doorway. "You two have my vote. Merry Christmas!" He blew Ashley a kiss and hurried down the hallway.

Chase and Ashley stood there for a beat, then Chase asked, "Can I come in?"

"Sure." She walked over to the table, set the chocolates on the nearby counter, and found a tall vase to put the flowers in.

Chase stood uncertainly next to the table full of food. "Hungry?"

"Starved," she admitted.

"Great. Me too. Shall we?"

"Sure." She sat and they uncovered the dishes. He said a quick prayer and they filled their plates with the variety of dishes. She took a bite of marinated chicken. It was delicious.

"Sorry our dinner was interrupted." His voice was cautious, testing the waters.

"Oh ... yeah. Sorry I left. I didn't want to interrupt."

He studied her as if wondering if she'd run again. She wasn't quite ready to discuss that yet. "So the Chadwicks are your family after all?"

He nodded. "Crazy, huh?"

"It actually fits perfectly now that I know." She tilted her head and studied him. "You look a lot like them and they're all impressive, hard-working, and successful. Like you."

"Thank you. They were more welcoming than I had hoped for. I'm excited to get to know them better."

It was probably hard for him to break away from his new family and come eat dinner with her. "So it went well ... meeting everyone?"

"Yes. It was great." He picked up a roll and broke off a piece. "Better than great, really. They're all like you said, really impressive. It's exciting to have brothers, a little sister, cousins, an uncle, and in-laws." His face got more animated. "Grams is the best. She already loves me like one of her own."

"I bet. She's an incredible lady."

"She is." He ate the bite of roll, then chuckled. "But she does want me to shave my beard."

"Don't." She said that simple word far too passionately for what they were discussing.

His gaze darted to hers. "You like my beard?"

"Yes," she admitted. The beard wasn't all she liked about him.

A slow grin grew on his face. "Okay, I won't."

She smiled and ate a bite of cauliflower. They ate quietly for a minute. She hated to stomp on his excitement about his family, but she had to know. "Did you pursue me so you could get an easy introduction to the Chadwicks?"

He set down his fork in surprise. "No. Not at all. I was planning to find Quill and talk to him, but I never saw him. I found out he's at a hockey game. I didn't want to upset the family before the weddings, so I stayed away yesterday. That's why I waited to approach any of them. Luckily, they came to me." He studied her. "You believe me?"

She paused and then nodded. "Yes. So was that your secret you were going to tell me?"

"One of them."

"And that's the reason you came to Mystical Lake. You didn't come to be with someone?"

His blue eyes registered confusion. "Well, my mom was gone and I got the information that they might be my family. I came to see if it was true or not. I had the time off. Some of my friends had invited me for Christmas, but I thought I might as well come and see if I could find my dad and siblings." He frowned. "Of course my dad isn't here, but my siblings, Grams, and everyone else more than make up for not meeting him."

So he wasn't here because of Kris. His secret had turned out to be something positive, and his family had welcomed him with open arms. Her secrets were still waiting to come out and she doubted they'd be as positive.

They ate and talked about each of his family members. She already knew and loved the Chadwicks, so it was fun to hear his take on them and talk about the ones who were famous like Cedar, Cruz, and Quill, Devon the super spy guy, and Dax the hilarious nephew.

"I love having a nephew," he said, grinning. "Do you have any nieces or nephews?"

"Yes." She nodded. "Two nephews almost as funny as Dax and a beautiful newborn niece."

"That's awesome. I'd love to meet them."

"That'd be fun," she said noncommittally. "So what did Dax say to you?"

Chase chuckled and started into the story of Dax trying to wrestle with him in the middle of the party and how funny he was. Ashley smiled and asked more questions, but the apprehension about the secrets she needed to tell Chase tied her stomach in knots. She couldn't eat anymore. She took sips of her water as Chase ate and talked, but then he abruptly stopped. "Why aren't you eating?"

"Nervous," she admitted.

Chase set down his fork and stood, taking her hand and grabbing two mints off the tray. He offered her one. She took it. The peppermint refreshed her mouth and calmed her stomach a bit. There was no hope for it to settle completely until she and Chase talked and she found out if he was willing to help her work through her commitment issues.

They walked to the couch and settled in side by side. Chase turned to her and said, "Do you want me to tell you my other secrets or would you like to go first?"

"I'd prefer gentlemen before ladies," she admitted. She was such a wimp, but it was nice to have a little reprieve.

He smiled gently, brushed her hair from her face and said, "My big secret, the one I hope you'll respond favorably to ..."

Ashley's stomach swooped and swirled. What if his secret was awful and drove her away? Well, at least then she wouldn't have to tell him about her lame marriage phobia and the worries about whether she could ever be in a lasting relationship.

"I want to date you Ashley. I want to be with you. I don't want to scare you away, but the time we've spent together—except when you're pushing me away—has been incredible for me. I think you're incredible." He took a deep breath and waited, studying her as he awaited her answer.

"Oh, Chase ..." She wanted to laugh and cry. That was his big secret? He wanted her and thought she was incredible. How in the world could she share her secrets now? "I don't even know what to say ... You're incredible too. I'm so impressed with you and I want to be with you, but—"

Chase shook his head, plucked her off the couch, and held her against his chest. Ashley's breath whooshed out and any desire to be apart from him, ever, fled. "We're going to pause for a moment and savor those words."

"What words?" She stared into his beautiful blue eyes and felt his minty breath against her mouth.

"You want to be with me. I'm going to convince you to never leave and then you can share your secrets."

Ashley couldn't think straight being so close to him. "How are you going to convince me never to leave?" No other man had been able to convince her. She was worried she was falling her pattern from each year of falling in love during the magical Christmas season but then waking up to reality after she planned her dream wedding.

"You said at the Newlywed Game that when I kissed you, you can't think straight." He grinned, mischievously and beautifully.

"That is true," she admitted, her breath quickening.

"Good. For the next few minutes, I don't want you thinking straight."

He lowered his head and their lips met. Ashley savored the connection, his soft, warm mouth on hers and his strong body close. She threw her arms around his neck and kissed him with wild abandon. Chase might have jerked in response, but he recovered quickly and met her kiss for kiss. She honestly wasn't sure how much time had passed when they came up for air and simply stared at each other.

Chase grazed her chin with his knuckles and said huskily, "If we just kiss all night, would that be okay with you?"

Ashley stuttered out a half-laugh and kissed him again. He wanted to be with her. This incredible man wanted to be with her. She wanted to laugh and sing and dance in circles. The kisses continued and she was happily content when Chase slowed the kissing down and simply held her against his chest. She rested her head in the crook of his neck and splayed her hands against the muscles of his chest.

"This should be a Christmas Eve tradition," she murmured.

"Kissing the night away?"

She nodded.

"I like it." He massaged her back but then stopped abruptly. "Wait. Did you just tell me in girl-speak that we're going to be together every Christmas Eve and we're beginning to make traditions right now?"

Ashley smiled, but reality quickly sobered her. "We still have to talk through my secrets." The word "secrets" was much better than admitting she had issues.

He held her tighter. "I can't imagine anything you have to tell me that would pull me away from you."

Ashley bit her lip and forced herself to slip out of his arms and onto her own cushion. Chase frowned, but didn't make an issue of it.

"On April 26th, I was supposed to get married," she said quickly. Now that she'd committed to tell him, she wanted it over with.

His eyebrows lifted.

"I planned the perfect wedding and thought I had the perfect groom. Until I walked down the aisle and dumped him."

Chase's brow furrowed. "He must not have been right for you." He paused and though she agreed, she also knew that wasn't the real issue. "I'm glad you didn't get married. You wouldn't be here with me."

She studied her hands and kept talking. "I thought if I actually got to the wedding, I might be able to go through with it." She licked her lips. "But last year was just the same as the six years before it."

She glanced up. He swallowed and said, "Six years before? What do you mean?"

"Every year close to Christmastime, since I turned twenty-one, I've met someone and fallen in love with them quick—or at least thought I was in love. Every time they talked me into a spring wedding." She studied her hands and said quietly, "Every time I've had the best time planning my wedding, but not the best experiences with my future grooms. I've broken off the engagement days, weeks, or months before I could go through with it. Well, except last time when I got to the wedding aisle before I ran."

Chase sat there, obviously stunned. When she looked at him, he said, "That's why you've fought me so hard. You didn't want to fall in love at Christmas again?"

All she could do was nod. She'd had the fears of him being a flirt and a player but she didn't believe that any longer.

"So you don't think what's between us is real or lasting?"

"I wouldn't say that, but you should be the one worried here. This pattern has repeated itself too many times. Honestly, I'm terrified that I'm a real-life Runaway Bride or something."

There was silence for a second and then he said, "So you have an issue with the wedding day. We can work through that. We can elope or do a destination wedding."

Her heart started racing and her palms felt clammy. He obviously wasn't listening. "The wedding isn't the problem. I am."

The only sound in the room was their breath. She couldn't look at him. "I've been falling for you because you're the most incredible man I've ever known." She wrung her hands together. "All the times I've pushed you away, it was for whatever excuse I could conjugate in my brain—usually that you're a flirt and a womanizer."

"You think I'm a flirt and a womanizer?"

"No," she admitted. "But the other men I've been engaged to were, so I told myself that you were the same so it wouldn't hurt so bad when I ran away from you."

His eyebrows lifted and he studied her. Taking her hand, he said softly, "You have some commitment issues. We can figure that out, Ashley."

She pulled her hand back and shook her head. "What I'm trying to tell you is that you're amazing, but I don't know that I'll ever be capable of a lasting relationship." Her voice dropped. "Even with someone as incredible as you."

Silence fell between them. When she couldn't handle it any longer, she looked up at him. His eyes were solemn and his face tight. A battle was raging behind those beautiful blue eyes of his. Finally, he seemed to make a decision and nodded. "Have I made it clear that you're the perfect woman for me and I'd do anything to be with you?"

Ashley's heart threatened to explode out of her chest. How could she not give herself to a man like this? Maybe if they eloped tomorrow, she wouldn't have time to think and stress and run. "Yes, you have."

He looked over her face carefully, then leaned forward and gave her a tender kiss. "I don't want to be premature about this, but I love you, Ashley."

She sucked in a breath.

He studied her. "And that means I won't pressure you to be with me." He stood and gazed down at her. "I love you. I think you're perfect. I'll do anything and work through any issue with you. When you're ready, you know where to find me."

With those awe-inspiring and terrifying words, he gave her one more tender gaze and walked purposefully to the door and out of the room.

Ashley deflated against the couch. She wanted to run after him, but she was afraid. Was she simply falling in love at Christmas again? Would she run once the wedding plans had been made? No! Chase was different. How she felt about him was different. He was the type of man she could be happy with forever.

But how could she be certain?

She rolled over onto her knees and, tears streaming down her face, she begged for help.

CHAPTER TEN

Chase slept miserably Christmas Eve night. He woke to his phone ringing. It was eight a.m. and barely light outside. He blinked and grabbed his phone, praying it was Ashley, but she didn't even have his number.

"Hi, Mom."

"Merry Christmas, handsome!"

"Merry Christmas to you."

"Oh, I wish we were together. How was Christmas Eve? How's your Christmas morning been? Who are you with? Did you talk to the Chadwicks? Was Peter there?"

He rolled off the bed with a groan. He didn't usually sleep in this late and it felt awful. He felt awful. Where was Ashley? Had she gone to Missoula to be with her family? He wanted to run down the hallway and bang on her door. He'd said she knew where to find him, but did she? Did she know his suite number? She definitely didn't know his address in Missoula. Maybe he should shove a slip of paper with all his information under her door for when she was ready to find him. Would that just shout how desperate he was to be with her?

"Hello? Are you there, love?"

"Sorry, Mom." He passed a hand over his face and strode to the window, pulling back the blinds. It was an incredible view of the lake, the mountains, the trees—a beautiful winter wonderland. "Things are good. Yes, I met most of the Chadwicks last night. Peter's gone. None of them see him." It was weird to call his dad Peter, but what else could he call him? The way the family talked about him, it was doubtful Chase would meet him anytime soon. "The rest of them were great. Welcomed me right in."

"Oh, love, that's wonderful."

"Thanks, Mom. They were all incredible, but Grams is amazing. She wants you to come meet everyone."

"Really?" Her voice was full of disbelief.

"Yeah."

"Peter's mom wants to meet me, the woman he cheated on his wife with?"

Chase flinched but kept his voice even. "Yes, Mom. They will all love you and you'll love them."

"I'll talk to Ned about it." Her voice was soft and uncertain. He didn't hear that very often from his mother. She was loving with him but never vulnerable.

"Okay," he said, not wanting to push too hard. This was all a lot for her to take in. It was still a lot for *him* take in. "I'd love to see you too."

"Ah, my boy. I miss you. You're the only reason it's hard to be away from that icy spot of earth."

He laughed.

"So you'll spend Christmas day with them?"

"Grams wants me to. They're all really welcoming, so I'm sure it'd be great." He didn't know how to tell her about Ashley, so he just spit it out. "But I've found someone, Mom, and I really want to spend the day with her." The rest of his days, truly.

"What!" his mom sputtered. "*You've* found someone. My too-handsome boy who's never going to give me grandbabies has found someone? Ned!" she shrieked. "Book us tickets to Montana. I don't care if we get frostbite. Chase is settling down."

Chase laughed though he hurt inside. "Slow down, Mom. You're welcome here any time, but I've got a lot of praying and talking to do before she'll settle down with me."

"Well, unless she's an idiot, she'll fall head over heels for you," his mom said indignantly.

He smiled. "Ah, Mom. Always thinking I'm better than I am."

"You're better than anyone," she insisted. "Now tell me about this girl."

Chase had no problem complying with that request. An hour later, he finally hung up the phone and went to shower. His mom was great, but she absolutely could not understand why he and Ashley weren't making wedding plans. He didn't tell her about Ashley's commitment issues or being engaged seven times before.

Seven. He could hardly wrap his own mind around that, and his mom wouldn't like it. Instead, he gently teased his mom about how long it took Ned to talk her into getting married. She laughed and agreed that Ashley could have a week or two to get her head on straight.

He showered, got dressed, and wrote his information out on

a pad of paper. His home and work address, his work and personal email addresses, his cell and work phone numbers, his suite number here at the resort, and that he'd be here until tomorrow night and then be back in Missoula and back to work by January second. It looked completely desperate, but he wrote on the bottom, *Any time, any day, any place ... I'll never stop praying for you to come to me. I'll never give up on you.*

He grasped the note as he slid into his coat and headed out the door. He'd spend Christmas Day with the Chadwicks ... if Ashley didn't respond to this note. He said a quick prayer then walked down the hallway, slid the note under her door, rapped on the wood frame softly, and waited. And waited and waited and waited.

He began to doubt, but he knocked harder. Worst case, she was in there and hiding from him, wishing he'd just go away. Best case, she was still asleep and as soon as she read his touching note and saw how desperate he was for her, she'd agree they could work through any issues together. Somewhere in the middle—she was out running or in the gym.

What if she'd gone home to Missoula? That was leaning toward worst case. Would she really run from the chance to work things out?

His phone rang and he jumped. Maybe it was her. Maybe she hadn't gotten ready yet, so she was calling him. Glancing at the caller ID, his hopes disappeared. Kris. He didn't want to talk to her. He wanted Ashley.

But Ashley wasn't around and he didn't want to be a jerk to Kris. The famous woman portrayed some beautiful sweetheart to the world, but she was obviously a complete mess, and her boyfriend was a loser.

He finally slid it over to green. "Hello?"

"Chase!" Kris wailed. "Oh, Chase! Please come ..." Her voice broke and she sobbed. "Please come help me. Please!" The last word ended in an ear-piercing squeal.

Chase sprinted toward the elevator. "Kris? Kris, I'm coming!"

She screamed so loud he was certain she couldn't hear him.

"Kris! Are you in immediate danger? I'm on my way. Do I need to call the police?"

She cried harder.

"Kris!" His alarm went up. "Answer me, please ... Kris!"

He opted for the stairs, figuring he could beat the elevator down.

"I'm not in danger," she finally gasped out between sobs. "But I need you, I need you!"

Chase's neck prickled, but he had always been the one to protect and help those who needed him. Maybe it was his doctor's instinct, or the military, or being raised by a very conscientious mom who taught him to be successful and help others rather than waiting for a handout.

He sent a quick text to Grams telling her he would be late. He wished he could be with Ashley, but that dream was moving further and further away.

———

Ashley woke to a soft rap on her door. She laid there, uncertain if she'd really heard anything. A louder rap came. She pushed the covers off and stepped out of bed, wondering who was at her door. Chase? That thought had her hurrying for the door. She yanked it open.

She saw Chase immediately. Instead of waiting for her to answer the door, he was rushing for the stairs. She heard him calling out to Kris. His voice sounded panicked. She watched him rush through the door and disappear.

Deflated, she stepped back into the room, but spotted a slip of paper on the floor. As she read his sweet note, her hopes inflated again. She wanted to call him immediately, chase him down and promise she'd never give up on him either.

Then she remembered he was going to help Kris.

She didn't know what to do. She sat staring out the window at the gorgeous Christmas morning. She wanted her family, especially her mom. She and her mom had struggled through teenage years and sometimes beyond that. Her mom didn't mince words about all the "lame" men Ashley had been engaged to. Throughout each of her engagements, she and her mom had been at odds. After Ashley gave the engagement ring back, it was always a little awkward with her mom. Every single time, her mom had been happily right that each of the men weren't right for Ashley.

Right now, she didn't care if her mom said she was stupid for falling in love at Christmas for the eighth time. She simply wanted to hug her, hug all of them, and be home. Maybe her mom would help her see the situation with Chase clearly. She'd probably tell her to dump him, just as she had the past seven guys Ashley thought she'd been in love with.

But Chase felt more real, more exciting, more perfect for her than any of the other men. Nobody else even came close.

She showered, packed, and hurried from the resort. Climbing into her Cherokee, she wished she could see Chase, but it was better if she just went home. She needed time to think and Chase needed time to help Kris. She shuddered as her vision filled with that beautiful, famous woman with her bosom spilling out of her robe. If Chase was anything like the other men she'd fallen for, Kris would definitely be too much to resist. Though she hated it, maybe this was a good test for both of them. He'd be back in Missoula tomorrow and hopefully they could work things out then.

She made it home in a little over an hour. The cheers as she walked in the house were a lift to be sure. She kissed and hugged everybody from her grandparents to her siblings and their spouses to her aunts and uncles and a variety of cousins. She chased her two wild nephews around and pinned them down for kisses amongst much protest and hollering, then she held her baby niece, Addie, for long enough that her sister-in-law finally begged for her baby back. The morning went quickly and she helped prepare Christmas lunch.

As she was chopping veggies for a salad, her mom sidled up close and said in a low voice, "What's going on with you?" She tilted her head and studied her daughter. "Did you fall in love at Christmas again? Seriously, honey."

Ashley couldn't hold her mom's gaze. She focused on the green pepper she was dicing, but tears blurred her vision. Oh goodness. If only she was chopping an onion. Then she'd have an excuse for her crying. She couldn't be crying. Her mom would have a conniption fit.

Raucous cheers sounded from the living room where the men were watching football while they were supposed to be watching the children. Her mom loved to cook and Christmas dinner was a huge event for her. She had stopped allowing men in her kitchen after Ashley's dad almost burned the house down making mac and cheese when they were little. No matter that one of Ashley's uncles was a chef. He was allowed to bring delicious appetizers that he made at his own home before the party.

"Ashley and I have to go see if that new dress I bought her fits," her mom announced to the aunts and her sisters-in-law.

They all nodded but looked on with interest as if they knew exactly what was happening. Whispers followed as she and her mom exited the kitchen, skirted the living room, and hurried to her mom and dad's bedroom where the dress hung. She could only imagine the uproar and teasing if she admitted she'd fallen in love at Christmas for the eighth time. But now as she thought of Chase and how perfect he was to her, and for her ... Were any of the other times even close to love? They all seemed empty in retrospect.

Her mom shut the door and tugged her over to the bed, sitting down on the edge and pulling her down with her. She studied her and then a smile blossomed on her face. "Oh my goodness, I have such a good feeling right now," she all but squealed.

Ashley stared into her mom's green eyes and shook her head, blinking back the tears, but a couple traitorous drops spilled over. "You do?"

"You're crying about a *man*."

"I've cried about a lot of men. Seven previous fiancés, to be exact."

"No, you haven't." Her mom jutted out her chin. "You've cried because your wedding plans that you worked so hard on didn't come to fruition. You never loved one of those cheating losers that you got engaged to. If you had listened to me, you would've dumped each of them on their butts before they even dared to propose. None of those idiots was worthy of you." She eyed her shrewdly. "Maybe you got engaged to each of them just to spite me."

"Come on, Mom." Ashley swiped at the tears on her cheeks, but they didn't stop.

She missed Chase. She wanted to be with him. Was he even now kissing on Kris?

No. Chase wouldn't do that. He'd told her he loved her, and she knew he meant it.

"I'm not a rebellious teenager anymore," she said to her mom. "I didn't get engaged to spite you. I wanted the fairy tale. I wanted what you and Daddy have."

"Um-hmm, that man of mine is a stud-muffin, isn't he? Whoo, he's hot."

"Mom!" Ashley blushed and stopped crying.

Her mom laughed heartily. "Life's not a fairy tale, honey. No matter that you create fairy tale weddings every day, that's not long-term reality. You can't replicate true love with a man who's not worthy of you. A man who doesn't know how to keep his lips locked with the right woman."

"I think I've figured that out." At least, she'd figured out how to get out of a bad relationship, but why was she running from Chase? She wanted to trust him and run to him.

Her mom tilted her head to the side. "But you're in love again. This time I think it's real."

Ashley bit at her lip and thought of Chase. His blue eyes. His kindness. His kisses. "He's incredible, Mom."

"Then why are you here?"

"Because it's Christmas and I love you."

"Ah, baloney. You're running. You didn't want to fall in love and get engaged at Christmas again, so you ran." She shook her head. "I can't believe I raised a wimp."

Ashley raised her eyebrows. "I am not a wimp."

"Hmm," was all she said, but then her eyes lit up. "Come on.

I'm letting your Aunt Suzy take over Christmas dinner. She thinks because Robert's a chef, she knows more about cooking than me. Bah! I need details, juicy ones, and I need them quick."

Ashley laughed and told her mom everything, starting with the first moment in Chase's office, which her mom thought was hilarious.

It felt good to share. If only she knew that she wasn't falling into her same pattern. If only she knew she could fully commit to Chase, that she wouldn't run when she should be walking down the aisle.

CHAPTER ELEVEN

Chase made it to the beautiful cabin Kris was renting on the southwest side of the lake and was greeted first by her black Great Dane, Pepper. Kris welcomed him inside wearing only her stupid bathrobe again.

She was a crying, sobbing mess because Aaron had left her on Christmas.

Chase made an executive decision to protect himself and hopefully calm her down. He told her he'd make breakfast while she showered and put on warm winter clothes that covered her completely. He was not here to be seduced by her; he was here to be her friend.

For a few seconds, she looked like he'd slapped her. Then, despite the fact she was still crying, she tried to flirt with him. He explained she could either put on clothes without any skin hanging out or he was leaving.

Surprisingly, she listened.

He cooked omelets and French toast and she came back into

the room looking much better. Thankfully, though her clothes were still skin-tight, there wasn't any flesh hanging out.

As he ate breakfast and she picked at hers, she started talking. She talked and cried and talked and cried some more. For hours. It was awful. Chase had learned to exhibit compassion throughout his training, residency, and days as a doctor, but he was being pushed to his limit. He kept hoping his phone would beep and Ashley would be on the other end, but he only got a couple of messages from Grams asking him to come as soon as he could.

Kris told him everything from childhood on up. She'd been neglected and "bought off" by her parents. She went on about every boyfriend she'd ever had, starting in the seventh grade. Then she got into the story of Quill and how kind and respectful he was. He was the only man she hadn't been able to seduce, and she'd never loved anyone like she loved him. He'd made her feel like she had value and a brain. When he broke up with her, she thought she was going to die. She admitted she'd been so into Chase and worked so hard to snare him because he looked like Quill and she missed Quill so much.

Chase didn't have to do much more than nod and mumble "hmm" occasionally, but her sordid affairs and her sad life started wearing on him. Crazy how she portrayed happiness, exuberance, and near-perfection on social media, but it was all fake.

If only he could be with Ashley. There was nothing fake about Ashley.

Kris explained how when she found the writer "Pepper" and it was the same name as her dog, she knew that was fate. She and Todd schemed how to get back at Quill for daring to dump her. They planned to take Quill down using Pepper, clearing Todd's name of accusations about gambling and throwing the game.

Chase was furious that she'd hurt his half-brother and destroyed the career of whoever this Pepper person was. He forced himself to hold his tongue and let her finish her story.

When she finally seemed to run out of tears and words, he cleaned up the spoiled food he'd left out and she sat there watching him. It was after two p.m. What a wasted Christmas day. He should be happy he could help someone on Christmas, but he doubted anyone could truly help this woman. She portrayed a positive, happy, kind vibe online, but she was a shriveled, selfish mess inside. Nothing he could say would change her or help her. The best thing he could do was tell Quill the truth and let his brother decide if he wanted to take action against her or not.

He finished cleaning up and walked back over to the table. "I, um, need to go. My family's expecting me for Christmas."

The tears started again. She sniffled. "I'm all alone for Christmas because I finally got my moxie up and dumped Aaron for the final time."

Chase was certain she'd said earlier that Aaron had dumped her, but he wasn't about to bring that up and get more tears.

Her dark eyes suddenly got a self-serving glint in them. "Can I come with you? I'll get all pretty and shiny and they'll love me. Everybody loves me and it'll be so much fun for your family to have a celebrity for Christmas."

Chase's eyebrows rose. "I don't think that's a great idea. You really want to spend Christmas with Quill Chadwick's family?"

"That's who you're going to be with?" Her eyes widened. He wondered how she hadn't connected the dots. She'd brought Chase here to meet Quill. She jutted out her chin. "I think they'll love me still."

He shook his head. "Not after I tell Quill that it wasn't all on

Todd Plowman. That you ruined Pepper's career and tried to ruin Quill's entire life."

She started crying again.

His phone rang. He yanked it out, praying for Ashley. It was Grams. Was he saved? "Hello?" His nerves and hopes ramped up. He walked away toward the open living area, Kris crying behind him.

"Chase! Where on earth are you, my boy? I've been waiting all of Christmas for you."

"Grams." He felt like home was on the other end of this line. "I'm wishing I was with you too. I'm dealing with a problem here."

"Oh, shoot. How long will you be?"

"I don't know. She's kind of an ..." he lowered his voice, "unstable mess." He looked over his shoulder.

Kris was wiping her eyes and glaring at him. How many tears could one body hold?

"It's Kris Bellissima," he admitted.

"Are you serious?" Grams's voice was full of shock. "I have some things to say to that woman."

"She wants to come with me to your house for Christmas."

"No. Seriously?" Grams paused and then found her tongue. "The nerve. The gall. The absolute audacity. She tries to destroy Quill and almost destroys Cora and she thinks she can show up for eggnog? Wow. I guess you have to admire the guts, right? Just a second, love." She paused and talked to somebody. "Okay, here's the deal. Drop me your location and Cora and I will be right there."

"Okay." He wasn't certain what Kris had done to Cora. He hoped he wasn't about to mediate a girl fight. Yes, Kris was a nightmare, but it was also Christmas. He wanted to be done with the drama. "Where's Quill?"

"Ren had some trouble on his wildfire. We've been praying hard and just got word he's okay, but Quill, Cedar, Aster, and Mavyn all went to him. I don't know when they'll be back."

He really wished Quill was here. Not only had Chase never met him, but he felt Quill deserved an apology from this woman. He deserved to decide what to do. "Okay, see you soon."

He ended the call and then shared his location with his phone. Turning around, he had no clue what to say to Kris until they got here.

She stood, her face lighting up. "We're going for Christmas?" She clapped her hands together.

"Um, no. Grams and Cora are coming here."

"What about Quill?" She stuck out her lower lip in a pout. "You understand he's my only true love, right?"

Yep, this was going to be a huge cat fight. Quill and Cora were dating now. Oh, boy. Should he tell Grams not to bring Cora?

"Um, I need to check on some things. Excuse me, please." He went out the front door and stood on the front porch. It was chilly out here, but much better than being stuck in the cabin with that woman one moment longer. Hadn't he done enough service today? Could he earn the blessing of Ashley coming to him for his good deeds? He'd settle for a text or a phone call or some encouragement. If only that's how good deeds worked.

He called Grams back, but it went to voice mail. He checked his phone to kill time, but there were only some texts from close friends and some of his staff wishing him Merry Christmas. He responded in kind.

A red sport utility pulled into the driveway. Cora, Hope, and Grams climbed out.

"Merry Christmas!" They all called cheerily to him. These women were his family, or in Cora's case, would be soon. They were good ladies, but would they be kind to the likes of Kris? She'd done a lot of damage to their family.

Grams gave him a tight hug, then he officially met Cora and gave her and Hope quick hugs.

"Chelsea wanted to come, but we figured this was no place for Dax. Luckily, Cat and Uncle Jay's crew are at his house doing some ice fishing for tonight's dinner." Hope lowered her voice. "You would *not* want Cat here. She's sassy. She'd tear that pampered Kris apart."

"What are you planning to do?" Chase asked. He knew Kris deserved a lot of angst for everything she'd admitted to him, but in her own way, she was suffering quite a bit. And besides, it was Christmas Day.

"Just a little humbling, but we'll be nice." Grams said. She walked around him. "As nice as we can be."

Chase hurried forward and swung the door wide. They filed inside. Kris wasn't in the living room or kitchen.

"Where do you think she went?" Hope asked.

They heard footsteps on the stairs and looked up. She'd obviously gone to primp. She had changed into tight jeans and a button-down shirt that didn't have nearly enough buttons done up. Her hair and makeup were far too much for Chase's taste. He preferred Ashley's simple beauty.

"Hi!" she called brightly as she descended the stairs, then her lip drooped. "Where are the men?"

"This isn't about men," Hope said. "We're her to support Chase and to talk about Quill and Cor—"

Kris reached the bottom step and her eyes popped wide as she turned to face Cora. "Pepper?" Her olive skin went a shade of pale gray and she backed up. "What are you doing here?"

"I'm Quill Chadwick's fiancée," Cora said, sweet as sugar, but her brown eyes flashed. "Isn't fate artistic?"

"No!" Kris squeaked. "No. Quill should hate you. He still loves me."

Grams looked to Hope. "I was planning on being kind, but she's pushing my buttons."

Hope smiled and turned to Kris. "Quill knows exactly how self-serving you are. You used Cora, as Pepper, just like you use people all over the place. The only miracle to me is that you haven't been exposed yet."

Kris regained her "moxie," as she called it, and tossed her long hair, giving them a snarky smile. "I'm very good at covering up messes."

"Well, you're not going to weather this one," Cora said. "Too many of us know that you are just as much to blame as Todd Plowman for the scandal with Quill and Pepper."

Kris looked away and her lower lip trembled. "I really am sorry, Pepper... I mean, Cora. I didn't mean to hurt you. You were just a means to an end."

Hope's eyes flashed and Grams grunted. "What end?"

"I love Quill, but he dumped me," she admitted. "Todd convinced me that I could humble Quill and he'd get back together with me."

Grams looked to Chase. "You know, I actually feel bad for her. She acts all perfect online, but she's pathetic."

"Ah!" Kris protested. She glared at Grams. "I'm not pathetic!"

Cora looked her over and took a deep breath. "Kris ... I want you to know that I forgive you."

Chase was impressed. Kris didn't deserve forgiveness but Cora was obviously a kind woman.

"You do?" Kris drew back in surprise. "Why would you forgive me?"

"Grams is right. I feel bad for you. Everything worked out in the end. Despite you trying to destroy Quill and I, we're together now and have never been happier."

Kris's lips turned down in an exaggerated pout. "I'm the one who's supposed to be happy with Quill," she insisted.

"I have the answer for you, and it's not Quill," Grams said. "Stop being selfish. Turn your heart to God and your life to helping others and you'll be happy."

Chase loved that. It sounded exactly like something his mom would've said.

Kris stared at her. "That's your answer? You people and trusting in a higher power." She wrinkled her nose. "Quill was always talking about junk like that too. I guess I should be glad Quill and I didn't end up together."

Cora's eyebrows lifted. "I think so too."

Kris flinched.

Chase hoped this was winding down. It would take more than inspiring words to help this woman. She needed extended therapy sessions with a very patient pastor or trained therapist.

"Here's what's going to happen," Hope said, obviously ready to be done with this conversation too. "You have two choices. First? You allow Mavyn to write an article exposing what you've done."

"Mavyn Vance?" Kris's eyes widened. "I love Mavyn Vance."

"Mavyn Vance is my best friend," Cora informed her.

"Ah ... crap," Kris muttered. "What's my other choice?"

Grams gave her a wide smile and finished for Cora. "Our

beautiful Cora survived the way you destroyed her career because she's a gifted suspense writer."

"Romantic suspense, thanks to Quill's inspiration," Cora interjected.

Grams laughed heartily at that as Kris's fake lips thinned. "Romantic suspense," she corrected and then gave Kris a compassionate look. "You will do a series of features on all of your sites with Cora, giving her loads of free book promotion. Cora and Hope will stay with you to get everything set up and uploaded right now. If any of them don't post on their scheduled dates, or if you ever try to hurt any of our family again, we'll assume you chose option one."

Kris stared at Grams as if wondering if she dared call her bluff. The staring contest didn't last very long before Kris muttered, "Okay."

Grams patted Cora on the arm. "We'll see you back at the house later. Come on, Chase."

Chase didn't need to be told twice. He took Grams's arm and hurried to the front door.

"Chase," Kris called after him.

Chase didn't want to stop, but he did, forcing himself to look back.

"Thanks for listening to me. For the record, you may be the only man besides Quill who resisted me." She winked. "That girl-friend of yours must be something special."

"She is," Grams said before Chase could respond. She tugged on Chase's arm and then they were blessedly out the door. It was like emerging from the viper's den.

Grams was surprisingly quiet as they drove to her house on the northwest side of the lake. There were a few cars in the driveway.

He got Grams's door and escorted her across the snow-packed drive and to the stairs. She patted his hand as they reached the landing. "That was very kind of you to try to help that awful woman this morning. I'm very grateful you didn't fall to her tricks."

"Thanks, Grams."

She grinned up at him. "I think the rest of your Christmas is going to be fabulous."

"Of course it will be. I'll be with my family."

She patted his cheek and let him open the door. The only thing that would make this Christmas better was to have Ashley appear, and of course for his brothers to come back. He was grateful Ren was safe and wanted to meet him and Quill.

They walked into a large open area. Chase loved the warm cabin-type feel and the huge windows overlooking the lake. Chelsea was in the kitchen stirring some kind of sauce on the stove. She waved happily as they walked in. "Merry Christmas!"

"You too!" he called back.

He heard a squeak of surprise and as he rounded the counter, he saw the little man Dax having an "airplane" ride with a lady's feet on his stomach. The woman lay on her back holding the boy aloft. Chase could see blonde hair and then she tilted her head back and smiled at him.

"Ashley!" He blinked and had to gasp for air. His chest felt tight and then expanded with the shock and joy of this Christmas miracle.

She set Dax down and he protested loudly, "Hey, it's not his turn. It's mine!"

Ashley scrambled to her feet, straightening her blouse and her hair and smiling shyly as Chase rushed across the living room to her.

Chelsea hurried over and lifted her son into her arms. "It's Chase's turn now. Let's look at your presents."

Grams appeared to be very interested in the sauce that Chelsea had left as Chelsea carried Dax over to a huge pile of toys. Chase and Ashley stood facing each other. He wasn't sure if he should talk first or let her, but he was so happy she was here. He could simply stand here and stare at her and already his Christmas would be a million times better than it had been.

"I'm so sorry," she said.

"No. You don't need to be sorry. I didn't want to push you." He lowered his voice. "I only want to be with you."

She stepped closer and happily they were almost touching. "My mom squared me up," she admitted. "She told me that I never loved any of my seven fiancés."

"Seven?" Grams interjected.

Ashley's face flared red. "It's a long story."

"You can tell us later." Grams waved a hand. "Sorry I interrupted. You can go somewhere private if you want, but I kind of like being your audience."

Chase didn't mind sharing this moment with Grams, but he looked to Ashley.

"I don't mind," Ashley said. "Because I actually am going to want to tell the whole world. I've fallen in love with Chase Hamilton. Fallen in love for real this time."

That was all Chase needed to hear. He wrapped her up tight, bowed his head, and kissed her. The kiss was full of the love they shared and the commitment that neither of them were going to back away from.

When they pulled apart, he rested his forehead against hers and just drank in the sight of her.

He heard Grams clapping happily. "You should do a spring wedding."

He felt Ashley tense.

"No," Chase said. "We're going to get married whenever and wherever Ashley wants."

She smiled tenderly at him. "I want to get married in the spot we fell in love, Mystical Lake, next Christmas."

"A year's engagement?" Grams questioned. "That's too long."

Chase smiled. "Ashley will need that time to plan her dream wedding. As long as I know she'll be mine, I won't rush her." He meant giving her time to work through any worries or commitment issues as much as he meant planning the wedding, and her eyes said she knew that. He dropped his voice. "Unless you want to elope on a tropical island next week?"

She smiled and tenderly kissed him. "I love the idea of my dream wedding at Christmas next year. But the more important detail is my dream groom. I love you."

"I love you. Merry Christmas."

Then they were kissing again. A year would be a long time to wait, but for Ashley he'd wait a decade if that's what she needed.

EPILOGUE

One Year Later

Ashley snuck a peek into the main open area of the resort. She couldn't see around the temporary barrier, but she could imagine Chase waiting up front, looking perfectly hand-some in his tux. Her dress was a tailored off-white gown with a pink tint under the tulle giving it a hint of color. It had a crystal-beaded waistband with jeweled buttons down the illusion back. The sparkling sequin lace appliques scattered over the bodice and skirt and the plunging illusion bodice completed the picture. It was breathtaking and every detail of their wedding would be perfect, but she didn't care. All she wanted was to be married to Chase.

Grams had been right. A year was a very long engagement.

"Get back in here," Grams demanded. "It's not time yet." She winked at Ashley's mom. "This girl is just chomping at the bit to race down that aisle."

Her mom laughed. "Good thing too. With her other engage-ments, she was racing the other direction."

Ashley smiled at their teasing. These two got along famously.

Chase's mom, Wren, poked her head into the bathroom. "Hi, sweet girl. You look gorgeous. You ready?"

"I can't wait a second longer," Ashley admitted.

Wren grinned. "Let's do this so I can fly back to Costa Rica and get out of this cold." She gave a fake shiver and they all laughed.

They filed out of the bathroom and to the barrier. Dax was ready, holding a velvet pillow with the rings. Chase's brothers were lining up to take their wives down the aisle behind the little guy. Grams was going to walk with Iris and Devon, Wren with her husband Ned, and her mom between both of her brothers. Her dad waited for her, grinning. She kissed his cheek, then tucked her hand in his elbow and waited, impatiently rocking from foot to foot.

"Are you going to bolt? Are you nervous?" her dad asked.

Ashley laughed. "No. I just want to be in Chase's arms already."

"Oh my. Forget I asked." Her dad's ears turned red and she laughed harder.

Dax led the way, uncharacteristically solemn. The other couples or trios moved down the aisle and finally, finally the bride's march started. She and her dad walked to the back of the aisle with friends and family standing and craning their necks to get a peek at her. She cleared the crowd and had a straight view of Chase. She sighed happily.

A big grin split his handsome face and his blue eyes twinkled at her. He hadn't shaved his beard, even for Grams. Ashley loved the short, dark hair shadowing his perfectly handsome face.

She hurried her pace. Her dad laughed and kept up with her. People started laughing as she ran on her heels, holding her dress in one hand, clinging to her dad, who was panting now.

Chase hurried down to meet her, swept her off the ground and into the air. He grinned up at her. "Running to me, beautiful?"

"Yes, sir." She laughed happily.

This was right. She would never run from Chase, only to him.

He lowered her to her feet and held her close, giving her a tender kiss.

"Come on, save it for after the ceremony," one of his brothers called.

"After the ceremony, we'll be running out of here to get to Tahiti," Chase murmured, giving her a seductive wink.

"And miss the fabulous wedding party I planned?"

"Okay, we can stay for dinner ... maybe."

She couldn't have cared less. The rest of the family could enjoy the dinner, the cake, the dancing. All she wanted was Chase.

He wrapped an arm around her waist and escorted her up to Pastor Brent. The friendly church leader was Chase's cousin-in-law, Meredith's dad. The man's dark eyes sparkled at him. Her father followed them and Pastor Brent had barely asked, "Who gives this lady away?" when a ripple went through the crowd.

She and Chase turned to see what was wrong. A man marched straight toward them, dressed in an off-white button-down shirt and tan slacks. His face was weather-beaten and he looked like he'd been traveling for a while. His blue eyes were eerily familiar.

"Dad?" Cedar spoke into the silence.

Chase tensed beside her.

Grams leapt up, rushed across the space, and smacked the man upside the head as if he was a small boy in trouble. "Peter, you stinking idiot," she cussed him.

"Hi, Mama," he said quietly.

Grams let out a heart-wrenching cry. Then she grabbed her son in a fierce hug, tears streaming down her face. "Oh, my boy, you've come home."

Nobody else moved or spoke. A tense silence filled the huge open area.

Grams pulled back, keeping a hand on his arm. "Well, start the apologizing. Make it good."

Peter grimaced. His eyes swept over his children, taking each one of them in. He only smiled briefly as his gaze lingered on Iris. None of them smiled back. Their expressions held varying degrees of shock and anger that he was here. His gaze stopped on Chase. Ashley could feel the angst radiating from her future husband. She wished she could make sure this man wouldn't hurt him.

"My plane got delayed. I didn't mean to do this," he said in a gravelly voice, gesturing around at the large wedding party. "I'm so sorry. I didn't do right by any of you." His gaze then traveled to Wren who simply watched him steadily, clinging to her husband Ned's hand, before going back to his children, focusing on Iris. "Days before your mom died, I admitted to her my ... indiscretion. She forgave me. Told me she knew something had been off that summer when I traveled to Missoula every weekend to research other hotels. But she had a newborn and was dealing with postpartum depression."

He cleared his throat. "Your mom loved me and forgave me, but it didn't make it right, didn't take away my pain of betraying her and hurting her, Wren, and Chase, not to mention all of you. I wanted to kill myself, but I couldn't do it. Lucy loved me too much and I knew that would hurt her. So I took off, ditched all of you the day of her funeral.

"I can't do anything to change it now, and I wish I hadn't messed up your wedding day." He nodded to Ashley. "But I needed to at least apologize." He looked at a loss for what else to say and finally muttered, "I'll go now." He bent and kissed Grams's cheek. "Love you, Mama."

Then he turned and started walking away.

Not even Grams moved. The room felt frozen.

"Stay," Chase said in a deep, aching voice.

Ashley glanced up at him. He was so handsome, so brave. Of course he'd forgive his father and ask him to be with them.

Peter whipped back around and blinked at Chase. "You want me to stay for your wedding?"

Chase nodded. "I want you to stay and be part of our lives."

Peter put a hand to his mouth. His weathered face crinkled as one tear escaped the corner of his eye and tracked down his cheek. "But ... the rest of you ..." He looked around at his children. "It's not right that I should betray your mother and then desert you and just ... come back." He looked so hopeful that Ashley wondered how any of them wouldn't take pity on him, but she wasn't a child that had been ditched by their father the day of their mom's funeral.

"Stay," Cedar said in a thick tone.

"Please stay," Aster inserted.

Quill and Ren both nodded, their gazes tight. They obviously weren't thrilled with their dad, but they wouldn't turn him away.

Iris let out a cry, pulled from her husband Devon's arms, and ran to her dad. He caught her easily, hugging her tight and saying over and over again in a voice choked with tears, "My girl. Oh, my beauty. My girl."

"Daddy." Iris pulled back and framed his face with her hands. "I've been so mad at you."

"I know." He broke down and couldn't speak. "I'm so sorry, beauty. I'm so sorry. You don't have to ever forgive me, but please know how much I love you, how I never stopped praying for you." He glanced around at his children. "All of you. I begged the Lord to bless and keep and prosper you while I loved you all from afar."

Grams let out a heart-wrenching sob. Ashley felt tears spilling down her own face. As she glanced around, she saw most of the wedding crowd was crying. She cuddled into Chase. He wasn't crying, but his blue eyes were very bright.

"Are you okay?" she asked.

He glanced down at her. "Of course I'm okay. I've got you."

She smiled and he gave her a soft kiss.

Peter escorted Iris back to Devon, shaking his son-in-law's hand and then giving each of his sons and their wives a hug. When he got to the front of the gathering, he hugged Chase tight and Ashley heard him whisper, "I'm so sorry I missed out on you."

"Our time isn't over," Chase said quietly.

Peter nodded to him, stepped back and offered his hand to Ashley. "Please forgive me for ruining your wedding day. You're a gorgeous bride."

"You didn't ruin it," she said. "We're glad you're here."

He gave her a grave smile and then escorted Grams back to her seat, hugging Uncle Jay, Cat, Cruz, and their spouses before sitting down.

"Wow," Pastor Brent said. "I don't think we're supposed to cry before the wedding starts."

"Only happy tears," Ashley said.

Chase wrapped his arm around her waist and pulled her in tight. "No tears," he insisted. "Only happy kisses. Excuse us for a few minutes, Pastor."

The crowd tittered as Pastor Brent grinned. "Kiss away. I'm here all day."

Chase turned her to him, bent down and kissed her tenderly. "I love you," he murmured against her lips. "Sorry if this isn't your perfect ceremony."

She dropped her bouquet and wrapped her arms tight around his neck. "I have you. All I care is to hear the words 'man and wife.'"

He grinned. "I also like 'you may kiss the bride.'"

"Let's do that part first then." And she kissed him, ignoring the cheering crowd and the wedding she'd planned for the past year. She was with Chase. That was all that mattered.

ALSO BY CAMI CHECKETTS

Mystical Lake Resort Romance

Only Her Undercover Spy

Only Her Cowboy

Only Her Best Friend

Only Her Blue-Collar Billionaire

Only Her Injured Stuntman

Only Her Amnesiac Fake Fiancé

Only Her Hockey Legend

Only Her Smokejumper Firefighter

Only Her Christmas Miracle

Jewel Family Romance

Do Marry Your Billionaire Boss

Do Trust Your Special Ops Bodyguard

Do Date Your Handsome Rival

Do Rely on Your Protector

Do Kiss the Superstar

Do Tease the Charming Billionaire

Do Claim the Tempting Athlete

Do Depend on Your Keeper

Strong Family Romance

Don't Date Your Brother's Best Friend

Her Loyal Protector

Steele Family Collection

Hawk Brothers Collection

Quinn Family Collection

Cami's Georgia Patriots Collection

Cami's Military Collection

Billionaire Beach Romance Collection

Billionaire Bride Pact Collection

Billionaire Romance Sampler

Echo Ridge Romance Collection

Texas Titans Romance Collection

Snow Valley Collection

Christmas Romance Collection

Holiday Romance Collection

Extreme Sports Romance Collection

Georgia Patriots Romance

The Loyal Patriot

The Gentle Patriot

The Stranded Patriot

The Pursued Patriot

Jepson Brothers Romance

How to Design Love

How to Switch a Groom

How to Lose a Fiance

Billionaire Boss Romance

Her Dream Date Boss

Fighting for Love: Return to Snow Valley

Other Books by Cami

Seeking Mr. Debonair: Jane Austen Pact

Seeking Mr. Dependable: Jane Austen Pact

Saving Sycamore Bay

Oh, Come On, Be Faithful

Protect This

Blog This

Redeem This

The Broken Path

Dead Running

Dying to Run

Fourth of July

Love & Loss

Love & Lies

ABOUT THE AUTHOR

Cami is a part-time author, part-time exercise consultant, part-time housekeeper, full-time wife, and overtime mother of four adorable boys. Sleep and relaxation are fond memories. She's never been happier.

Join Cami's VIP list to find out about special deals, giveaways and new releases and receive a free copy of *Seeking Mr. Debonair: The Jane Austen Pact* by clicking here.

cami@camicheckett.com
www.camicheckett.com

ONLY HER HOCKEY LEGEND

"Beautiful view," a deep voice said from her right.

Cora whirled to see who was speaking, and dropped her glass of juice. It hit the floor, shattered, and sprayed juice and glass shards all over her dress and Quill Chadwick's pants. She may or may not have let out a mild swear word. "Pelican pellets!"

Quill smirked and raised an eyebrow at her, probably because of her odd curse word. He wrapped a strong arm around her waist and easily lifted her away from the mess. Cora's breath whooshed out of her and she felt hot all over from the warm the pressure of his arm around her waist, his palm cupping her hip, and the incredible smell of his musky cologne.

She stared into his blue eyes and felt slightly faint. They were a beautiful true-blue, and they were completely concentrated on her. He was big, almost six-five and two-eighty. She knew all of his stats and far too much about him, most of it the lies produced by Kris Bellissima. Lies that unfortunately Cora had shared with the world. If he knew who she truly was he definitely wouldn't be gifting her with that appealing grin of his and keeping his arm securely around her waist.

Some employees whisked over and started cleaning up the mess, distracting her from his gaze. "I'm so sorry," she said to them.

"Oh, it's no problem, ma'am," a beautiful blonde smiled sweetly at her.

"Thank you."

Quill put just the right amount of pressure on her hip to direct her farther away from the disaster she'd made and the eyes of the crowd who had noticed her awkward moment. He took her around to an alcove of one of the restaurants that was thankfully quiet at the moment as all of the guests of the wedding parties and the resort were at the welcome party. The plan was a wedding each of the next three days and then a big Christmas Eve celebration.

He released his grip on her and turned to face her. She wished he hadn't stopped touching her but that was silly. She didn't know him and as soon as he found out who she was this conversation would be over. She and Mavyn had no pictures of them attached to their articles, simply a caricature that looked faintly like them, so maybe if she escaped soon he'd never know who she was.

"I'm sorry about your pants," she murmured, looking down at his now apple juice decorated navy-blue suit pants.

"I'll clean up just fine," he said.

She looked over his handsome face and admitted, "Yes, you do ... look fine."

"I could say the same."

Her face flared red but luckily her deep-brown skin wouldn't reveal that to him. "I thought hockey players were supposed to be covered in scars and missing teeth."

He flashed her a devil-may-care grin. "I've got a fabulous dentist and the suit covers the scars."

"For the sake of Thor's hammer." She fanned her face.

"What?" he asked, all beautiful innocence.

"Nothing." But she couldn't stop picturing his suit and dress shirt off and her examining each of his scars while he told her the story of each one. *Please help my stray thoughts*, she prayed, sadly without much faith. Her mama and daddy watching her from heaven would not be pleased.

"You know who I am?" he asked.

"Of course." She looked him over. "Everybody knows who Quill Chadwick is. You're a household name, a legend."

He chuckled and she loved the low, deep tenor of it. "No, I'm not."

"To hockey fans you are."

"Oh." His slow, sexy grin seemed to light her up. "And are you a hockey fan, Miss ..."

"Cora, Cora Nelson." She stuck out her hand as it seemed the proper thing to do.

His grin widened and he took her hand in his and held it. "Nice to meet you Miss Cora Nelson. You're a hockey fan?"

She took her hand back, though she didn't want to. "Yes, I am."

"What's your favorite team?" He folded his arms across his chest and casually leaned against the restaurant entry, as if he had all day to talk to her. He looked so appealing, confident, and comfortable she wished she could bottle the tough-guy elegance he radiated. Was that an oxymoron? Tough guy and elegant? It sure fit Quill Chadwick.

"Boston Bruins," she replied, trying to hide her smile. She did love the Bruins but she loved the Avalanche too. "Josh Porter is the toughest man I know."

He tilted his head and then shook it. "He knows how to throw a punch that's for sure." He touched his jaw as if remembering. "How do you know Josh?"

"I inter ..." Her mouth clamped shut. She'd interviewed Josh a couple of years ago as Pepper. She did not need Quill to put two and two together. He'd probably make sure she was kicked out of the wedding party and the valley. Not that Quill had ever attacked her or even Kris. He'd been a class act on every talk show Cora had watched him on as her own career dissolved when Kris claimed her own innocence and Pepper took the fallout with the American public. Luckily Todd Plowman had gone to prison.

"Excuse me," she managed. "I was interested in him back in college."

He nodded. "You went to UMass?"

"No, Harvard." She smiled weakly. At least she could tell the truth about college. What had Mavyn gotten her into and why had she agreed? She hated lying and here she was going to have to lie to him about everything. *Please forgive me*, she asked all of her heavenly parents. "Close by though."

His brow wrinkled and she wondered if he knew they were over an hour and a half driving distance, but he didn't say anything. "Bruins, huh?" His gaze went slowly over her face. "I guess everybody has to have one fault."

She needed something to lean against as her legs went weak with the power of that glance. She stuttered backward and came up with nothing, almost tripping off her own heels. Quill darted across the space between them and grabbed her around the waist. Her hands grasped his firm arms and she was having a hard time breathing being so close to him. The one man that she could never allow herself to be interested in seemed to be the very man who made her heart race, her body long to be closer to, and her mind want to flirt with. Fate definitely had a wry sense of humor.

————

Keep reading *Only Her Hockey Legend* here.

HER BILLIONAIRE BOSS FAKE FIANCE

Slipping on a patch of black ice, Lexi cried out, wind-milled her arms, and skidded over the asphalt. She prayed she wouldn't fall. The low thrum of an engine rolled over her as a single headlight flashed across her vision. Lexi screamed, horrified to see a motorcycle flying right at her. She was still skidding on the ice, trying to stay upright. If she fell, the motorcycle would run her over without even seeing her until it was too late. She shuffled on the ice, trying desperately to get out of the way and hoping her waving arms might warn the driver.

The cyclist must've seen her and clenched the brakes hard, because she heard a yell and saw the huge bike lift onto its front tire. Then the motorcycle hit the patch of ice, and Lexi launched herself out of the way as it skidded onto its side. Her feet slid out from under her and she hit the ice with her knees and hands. Pain spiked up her arms and thighs. She felt a rush of wind, and then—miraculously—the motorcycle skidded past her, metal screeching against ice and asphalt. The machine slid to a stop at the curb twenty feet away, minus its rider, who lay sprawled on the cold asphalt, not far from Lexi.

"No, no, no!" Lexi cried out. She crawled across the patch of ice, praying the person wasn't dead and praying no other vehicles came along and finished them both off.

She reached the man, who was dressed in a navy-blue suit that even a girl from Montana could guess was worth thousands of dollars. The suit was tailored perfectly for his large frame. Thankfully he wore a helmet, and she couldn't see any blood or bones poking out. Lexi shuddered. He was lying on his side, facing away from her.

"Oh no! Please don't be dead!" She glanced up at the heavens and called, "Please, Lord, don't let him die." There was no time for folding arms and decorum when a man's life was hanging in the balance.

The man in question groaned and rolled over onto his back.

"Sir?" Lexi touched his shoulder with her gloved hand, breathing a sigh of relief. At least she wasn't responsible for his death. "Sir, are you okay?"

"Not dead yet," he muttered. He undid his chin strap and pulled off his helmet.

Lexi gasped. Staring up at her was a handsome face she'd recognize anywhere: deep brown eyes, dark hair, tanned skin, and short facial hair that only enhanced his good looks. One of the famous Hawk brothers. America's Most Eligible Bachelor. The most handsome man in existence. Her new boss.

"Callum Hawk," she breathed out.

He arched an eyebrow at her and pushed to a seated position, then stood. At least he didn't move like he was broken. He tucked his helmet under his left arm and offered his right hand to her. "We should probably get out of the street in case any other crazies are awake this early." He flashed her the trademark smile that had women across America needing blood pressure medication.

Lexi took his gloved hand and let him pull her up. She was glad they were both wearing gloves, because the surge of energy that went through her simply being this close to him wasn't smart to experience with anybody's boss, let alone a new employer who didn't even know who she was. She'd just made Callum Hawk crash his motorcycle. Jiminy Christmas, she was in trouble!

He released her hand, wrapped his arm around her lower back, and guided her out of the street toward his motorcycle as if they were on a summer stroll through Central Park. Her heart raced out of control. Callum Hawk had his hand on her sweaty back and she'd wrecked his motorcycle. This was not good. She was going to get fired before she even set foot in his office. How would she help her family if she got fired?

"Are you damaged?" Her words came out too breathy and too high-pitched, as her throat was closing off. The motorcycle accident was her fault, but when she died of heart failure from his tingly touch, it would be all on him. "Shouldn't we call 911?"

Callum glanced down at her, his dark eyes filled with concern. "Do you need medical attention?"

"No." She pushed the word out, shocked that his first worry was for her. "But I just made you crash your bike, skid across the asphalt, and most likely ruin that beautiful Armani suit."

He chuckled, stopping next to his tipped-over motorcycle. "It's Brioni."

Lexi's eyes widened and she swayed on her feet. Brioni suits were at least quadruple the price of Armani. "Did it get ripped?" she demanded.

Callum grinned down at her. "I don't care. I only care if you're all right." His voice deepened, and she was so smitten by him in this moment she could barely keep on her feet. Callum Hawk—*the* Callum Hawk—cared if she was all right?

———

Find *Her Billionaire Boss Fake Fiance* on Amazon.

Made in the USA
Middletown, DE
11 July 2021

43968198R00096